Philip AND THE *Others*

Other novels by Cees Nooteboom

Rituals
A Song of Truth and Semblance
In the Dutch Mountains

Philip AND THE *Others*

A Novel by
Cees Nooteboom

Translated by
Adrienne Dixon

LOUISIANA STATE UNIVERSITY PRESS
Baton Rouge
1988

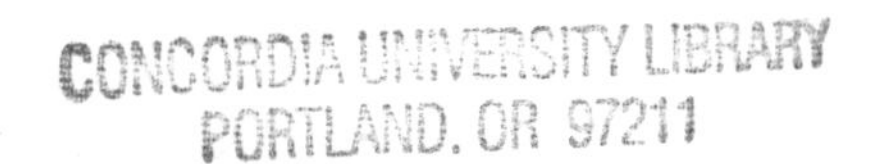

Originally published in the Netherlands in 1954 by Querido's Uitgeverij
as *Philip en de anderen*

Manufactured in the United States of America

97 96 95 94 93 92 91 90 89 88 5 4 3 2 1

Designer: Laura Roubique Gleason
Typeface: Aldus
Typesetter: The Composing Room of Michigan, Inc.
Printer: Thomson-Shore, Inc.
Binder: John H. Dekker & Sons, Inc.

Library of Congress Cataloging-in-Publication Data
Nooteboom, Cees, 1933–
[Philip en de anderen. English]
Philip and the others : a novel / by Cees Nooteboom : translated by Adrienne Dixon.
p. cm.
Translation of: Philip en de anderen.
ISBN 0-8071-1376-X (alk. paper)
I. Title.
PT5881.24.055P513 1988
839.3'1364—dc19 88-1394
CIP

The paper in this book meets the guidelines for permanence and durability of the Committee on Production Guidelines for Book Longevity of the Council on Library Resources. ∞

Preface

A long time ago, an eternity of over thirty years, a young man with whom I share a first and a last name sat down in the municipal library of a provincial town in the Netherlands. He was going to write this book. By the uninterrupted machinations of time I have stopped resembling him; and when they show me a photograph of this thin, romantic stranger, I am aware of the cruel distortion of his youthful features that has become my face.

He, in his day, had already been marked by the chaos of war and a medieval upbringing in an Augustinian monastery school; but somehow he had managed to keep a dream intact that had nothing to do with his, or with Dutch, outward reality. The dream would briefly find form in that library over a few months, as if it were dictated by an instance that would never have a name.

The book came out, and in his country he was from then on called a writer. He was probably the only one who realized that this would remain his only book for a long time. The reality of that summer in 1954 did not, or so it seemed, wholly correspond with his dream. Only much later, after he had traveled about the world for many years and in many capacities, would he write another book, and then many others.

When, while he was on his way to becoming the unavoidable me that I am, people mentioned his first book to him, he felt uneasy, as if it were not really his. He avoided reading it just as one sometimes refuses to look at an old photograph of oneself, not out of fear or mourning, but simply because the mystery of time's passage has become too perplexing. The book, like the photograph, would reject the forever-lost blend of impossible innocence, dreampower, and blissful inexperience. When he nevertheless glimpsed a page or a paragraph, he was astonished by his extreme visibility. He had not been worldly enough to hide, and now he preferred to ignore the young stranger who had written this book and to think of him as an improbable prehistoric self that somehow had managed not to die but to claim admission into his later life.

Then, after all those years of neglect, the young man wandered into a classroom in California, on the other side of the world, where a group of students of his own age listened to an old man of fifty-three speak almost apologetically about the book they both had written. But this time the young writer had allies. When the older man claimed "the barbaric time lapse" as his reason to ignore the book in favor of his later works, the students turned on him and explained his book to him. They told him he had no right whatsoever to censure the young man, that it was no longer his affair, that they wanted the young man to publish his book in their language, and that he, their teacher, was far too old anyway to understand such a book. They quoted names and phrases that he vaguely remembered from the book, and he was both ashamed and pleased. Something had somehow survived all those years, and now that unnameable something was given back to him by young eyes and young voices. They could do nothing to redeem the loss of irretrievable time, but among their voices he heard the one, unmistakable voice that once, in a long-forgotten Dutch summer had, out of an apparent nothingness, begun a tale with the words "My uncle Antonin Alexander was a strange man."

Berkeley, California
December, 1986

Pour Nicole et pour notre ami aux cheveux gris

Ces povres resveurs, ces amoureux enfants
—Constantijn Huygens

Je rêve que je dors, je rêve que je rêve
—Paul Eluard

Book One

1

My uncle Antonin Alexander was a strange man. When I saw him for the first time, I was ten years old and he was about seventy. He lived in an ugly, immensely large house in the Gooi, crammed with the most peculiar, useless, and hideous furniture. I was still very small and couldn't reach the bell. I did not dare to thump on the door or rattle the letter box, as I always did elsewhere. In the end I walked around the house. My uncle Alexander was sitting in a sagging armchair of faded purple plush, with three yellowed antimacassars, and he really was the strangest man I had ever seen. On each hand he wore two rings, and only later, after six years, when I went there for the second time, and then to stay, could I tell that the gold was brass and the red and green stones ("I have an uncle who wears rubies and emeralds") were colored glass.

"Are you Philip?" he asked.

"Yes, Uncle," I said to the figure in the chair. I saw only his hands. His head was in the shade.

"Have you brought me anything?" the voice asked again. I hadn't and I said, "I don't think so, Uncle."

"A visitor ought to bring something."

I don't think I found that odd at the time. It was true—a visitor ought to bring a present. I put down my suitcase and walked back to the street. In the garden next to my uncle Alexander's I had seen rhododendrons, and I cautiously entered the gate and cut off a few blooms with my pocketknife.

For the second time I was standing by the terrace. "I brought you some flowers, Uncle," I said. He stood up and at last I saw his face.

"I appreciate that very much," he said, making a small bow. "Shall we have a celebration?" He did not wait for my reply and pulled me by the hand into the house. He switched on a small lamp somewhere so that the peculiar room was lit by a golden light. The center of the room was full of chairs, and along the walls were three sofas covered with soft beige and gray cushions. Against one wall, from which doors opened onto the terrace, stood a kind of piano that I later learned was a harpsichord.

He made me go to a sofa and said, "Lie down. Take as many cushions as you like." He himself lay down on another sofa along the wall opposite mine, and then I could no longer see him because of the tall backs of the chairs between us.

"We must have a celebration," he said. "What do you like to do?"

I liked reading and looking at pictures, but you can't do that for a celebration, I thought, and so I didn't suggest it. I reflected for a moment and said, "Riding on a bus late in the evening, or in the night." I waited for an acknowledgment but none came. "Sitting by the river," I said, "and walking in the rain and sometimes kissing somebody."

"Whom?" he asked.

"No one I know," I said, but that was not true.

I heard him get up, and he walked over to my sofa. "We're going to have a celebration," he said. "First we'll go to Loenen on the bus and then back as far as Loosdrecht. There we will sit by the lake and perhaps have something to drink. Then we'll take the bus back home. Come along."

That was how I got to know my uncle Alexander. He had an old, whitish face in which all the lines ran downward, a fine, narrow nose, and thick black eyebrows, like frayed old birds. His mouth was long and pink, and usually he wore a yarmulke, although he was not Jewish. I think he had no hair underneath the cap, but I am not altogether sure. That evening was my first real celebration ever.

There were hardly any people on the bus, and I thought a bus in the night was like an island on which one lived almost alone. I could see my face in the windows and hear the soft talking of the people, like colors, above the sound of the engine. The yellow light of the small lamps made the things inside different from those outside, and the windows vibrated because of the cobblestones. As there were so few people, the bus hardly ever stopped, and I could imagine what it must look like from outside as it moved along the dike with its big eyes in front, the yellow rectangles of the windows, and the red lights at the back.

My uncle did not sit next to me; he went to a faraway corner, "because otherwise it won't be a celebration any longer, if you have to talk to each other," he said. And that is true. When I looked in the window behind me, I could see his reflection. It looked as if he were asleep, but his hands moved about on the little suitcase he had brought with him. I would have liked to ask him what was in the suitcase, but I thought he would probably not tell me.

In Loosdrecht we got off and walked until we came to the lake. There my uncle Alexander opened the suitcase and took out an old piece of canvas that he spread out on the wet grass. We sat down facing the moon, which quivered greenly in the water before us, and we could hear the shuffling of cows in the meadows on the other side of the dike. Strands of mist hung above the water, and there were strange little noises in the night, so that at first I did not notice that my uncle Alexander was perhaps crying softly. I asked him, "Are you crying, Uncle?"

"No, I'm not crying," he said, and then I was sure that he was, and I asked him, "Why aren't you married?" But he said, "I *am* married. I am married to myself." He took a drink from a small flat bottle he carried in his inside pocket (Courvoisier, the label said, but I didn't know how to pronounce it then) and he continued. "I *am* married. Have you ever heard of Ovid's metamorphoses?" I had never heard of them, but he said it didn't matter because they didn't really have much to do with it anyway.

"I am married to myself," he said again. "Not to myself as I used to be, but to a memory that has become me. Do you understand that?"

"No, Uncle."

"Good," he said, and he asked me if I liked chocolate. But I didn't, and so he ate the bars he had brought for me.

Together we folded the canvas into a small rectangle again and put it into the suitcase. We walked along the dike back to the bus stop, and when we reached an area of houses, we smelled jasmine and heard the water lapping gently against the rowboats by the jetty. At the bus stop we saw a girl in a red coat saying goodbye to her boyfriend. I saw her put her hand around his neck with a quick movement and pull his head toward her mouth. She kissed him on the mouth, but only briefly, and then she quickly climbed into the bus. When we entered after her, she had already become somebody different. My uncle sat down beside me, and so I knew that the celebrations were over. In Hilversum the conductor helped him get out, for he had grown tired and he looked very old.

"I'll play for you tonight," he said. It had become quite dark and the street was very quiet. "How play?" I asked, but he didn't reply. He didn't really take much notice of me any longer, not even when we were at home again in the living room.

He sat down at the harpsichord while I stood behind him and watched his hand turn the little key twice and then lift the lid. "Partita," he said—"symphony"—and he began to play. I had never heard such music before, and I thought only my uncle Alexander could play like this. It sounded like long ago, and when I lay down on my sofa again, it seemed very far away. I could see all kinds of things in the garden, and it was as if everything belonged to the music and to my uncle Alexander's soft sniffing.

From time to time he suddenly said something. "Saraband!" he called out. "Saraband." And later, "Minuet!"

The room became filled with the sound, and I wanted him never to stop, if only because I knew he was going to. When he stopped, I heard him panting. He remained still for a while, but then he stood up and turned toward me.

His eyes sparkled and they were very large and dark green, and he fluttered his large white hands. "Why don't you get up?" he asked. "You should get up." I stood up and walked toward him. "Here is Mr. Bach," he said. Although I saw no one else, he most certainly did, for he laughed strangely and introduced me: "This is Philip. Philip Emmanuel."

I didn't know I was called Emmanuel, but they told me later that when I was born, my uncle Alexander had urged that I be given that name because it was the name of one of Bach's sons. "Shake hands with Mr. Bach," said my uncle. "Go on, shake hands." I don't think I was afraid. I held out my hand and pretended to be shaking a hand. On the wall I suddenly noticed an engraving of a fat man with masses of curls, who looked at me kindly but from very far away. J. S. Bach, it said underneath. "That's right," said my uncle, "that's right."

"May I go to bed now, Uncle?" I asked, for I was very tired.

"To bed? Yes, of course. We must go to sleep," he said, and took me to a small room with yellow flowery wallpaper and a very old iron bedstead with brass knobs. "There's a chamber pot in the gray bedside cabinet," he said, and left. I fell asleep at once.

The next morning I was awakened by the sun warming me through the glass. I did not move, for there were so many new things to look at. Near me on the bedside cabinet stood the rhododendrons I had picked for my uncle the evening before. They had not been there last night, I was sure; he must have put them there while I was asleep. On the walls hung four objects.

One was a newspaper clipping neatly cut out and pinned up with four brass thumbtacks. It had turned quite yellow, but I could still read it clearly. It said: DEPARTURE LIST AND POSITIONS OF SHIPS—12 SEPTEMBER 1910. Beside it hung an old print behind glass, in a black lacquered frame. Dust had crept between the print and the glass so that the colors had softened. RETURN FROM SCHOOL it said, and it showed a boy in knee breeches and a broad-brimmed hat, jumping out of a coach drawn by two horses and running toward his mother, who stood waiting for him at the door, with open arms. In the garden around the house there were big yellow and blue flowers of a kind I had never seen in reality.

On the other wall hung a swimming diploma: BREAST-STROKE AND BACK-STROKE, CERTIFICATE A. In thin, pointed letters someone had written on it, "Awarded to Paul Sweeloo." Close above it hung a large faded photograph, mounted on cardboard, of a Eurasian boy with very large eyes and his hair in a fringe on his forehead, like mine.

I slowly got out of bed to go downstairs. The room gave onto a large landing lined with many more doors. I listened at each one to find out if my uncle was in any of the rooms, and I also tried to peer through the keyholes, but I couldn't see anything. With both hands on the banisters I went down the stairs and looked around the hall. It was very quiet in the house, and I was slightly afraid, for I couldn't remember which of the doors was that of last night. So I took my pocketknife, opened it out, and laid it flat on the parquet floor of the hall. Then I made it spin around very fast and waited for it to stop. There were doors on all sides, and whichever one my knife pointed to I would enter.

It turned out to be the door to the room with the sofas, for when I had very slowly pressed the door handle and the door was ajar, I heard my uncle sleeping. He was lying on the sofa fully dressed, with his mouth open and his knees slightly drawn up. His arms hung limply down so that his hands touched the floor. I could clearly distinguish him now and saw he was wearing a black jacket and pants without cuffs—striped pants of the sort that people wear when they get married or when they go to a funeral or when they are very old like my uncle Alexander.

Because I was afraid he might wake, I shut the door again, slowly, so that the lock would not click, and returned to my room upstairs. And there I found the books, Paul Sweeloo's books. There weren't many, and I could not yet read the titles of most of them; but six years later, when I slept in the same room, I wrote them down. The first one in the row was *Deutsches Jahrbüchlein für Zahnärzte 1909.* On the flyleaf it said, "To Paul Sweeloo, from . . . ," but I was unable to read the rest. Next was one volume of the collected works of Bilderdijk, "To Paul Sweeloo from Alexander, your friend." I could not figure out how that book got to be there, for, I thought, if you give a book to someone, surely you don't keep it yourself. The next one was *Kritik der reinen Vernunft* by Immanuel Kant, "To Paul Sweeloo, from your affectionate . . . ," and again I was unable to read the name.

So it went on. *Histoire de la Révolution Française,* seven volumes, by Michelet; *The Great Ages of Architecture,* by Henri Eevers; *Le Rouge et le Noir* by Stendhal; the *Letters* of Conrad Busken Huet, edited by his wife and his son; and finally, a tiny, very old book, *Dell'Imitatione di Christo di Tomasso da Kempis.* In all the books it said invariably, "To Paul Sweeloo," but the names after "from" were illegible.

I looked at the photograph as if for help, but the dark boy looked at me strangely, and suddenly I realized they were his books. Are you Paul Sweeloo? I wondered, replacing them on the shelf so that their backs formed a perfect, even row. When I had finished, I noticed that my hands were covered with thick gray dust.

On the bottom shelf of the bookcase stood a large box, and since the eyes of the portrait could not spy upon me as I crouched, I carefully lifted the cover. It was a record player. A record was still lying on the turntable—*Die Gralserzählung,* an aria from *Lohengrin,* by Richard Wagner. Beside the record lay a handle that had to be attached to the outside of the box and then turned in order to obtain music. I fanned the dust from the record with my handkerchief and started turning the handle. The music was harsh and angrily took possession of the room as if I were no longer there.

The record was playing so loudly that I did not hear my uncle Alexander until he was close to my door. Running in and gasping, he shouted, "Turn it off. Take that record off!" He pushed me aside and with a wild and even frightened movement he gave the heavy playing arm a shove so that the needle raked across the record and the music screeched to an abrupt halt.

My uncle paused until he caught his breath, and then he carefully, almost timidly, picked up the record and took it to a corner. "A scratch," he muttered. "There's a scratch on it now." As if it were merely dust, he tried to wipe the scratch away with his shirt sleeve. I removed the handle from the side of the record player and put it into the box. Then I went downstairs.

Out in the street, children were playing. From the terrace I could hear them calling, "Who wants to play witches? Who wants to play witches?" I could see them clearly through the bushes behind the fence. There was a suntanned girl with very long light-blonde hair and a light-blue sleeveless dress. The boy was small and had a narrow, old face with gray eyes. He walked with a limp. When the girl reached the part of the fence where I was standing, I came out of the bushes and said, "I'd like to play but I don't know the game."

"Who are you?" she asked.

"Philip Emmanuel."

"That's a silly name," said the boy, who had come closer, "and you can't play with us because you have girl's hair."

"I haven't," I said, "because I'm a boy."

"You have," he said, and he started singing in a whining tone:

> Philip has girl's hair,
> Philip is cra-zy,
> Philip can't play-ay.

"Don't be silly," said the girl. "Stop it. He can play if he wants to."

"He can't."

"Go away," she said, and to me, "Are you coming?"

"Where to?" I asked.

She raised her eyebrows very high and her eyes became very large, and she said, "To Africa, of course."

"But that's much too far away."

"Oh, stupid," yelled the boy. "Africa isn't far at all. It's just around the corner, on the next street."

"Shut your mouth," said the girl. "Shut your big mouth."

"Are you coming?" she asked me, and I climbed over the fence and walked along the street with her.

"If he's coming, I'm not," shouted the boy crossly. "Because he has girl's hair and he doesn't even know where Africa is."

I don't have girl's hair, I wanted to say, and I do know where Africa is—around the corner, on the next street.

She announced, "He *is* coming," and we walked off together. The boy remained by the fence and shouted, "Philip goes with Ingrid! Philip goes with Ingrid!"

We did not look back and I asked her, "Is that true?"

"I don't know," she said. "I'll have to think about it. Around the next corner is Africa."

It was a piece of land on which houses would shortly be built, for there was a big notice: HOUSES TO BE BUILT HERE FOR SALE. Ingrid spat at the notice. "Stupid sign," she said. The ground was full of holes, and there was a big pool with slimy light-green water plants growing in it. Elsewhere there were patches of gray, hard sand and a small hillock of greasy yellow soil—loam I think—and also bushes; sharp, tall grass; hogweed; and buttercups. Ingrid walked ahead of me down a narrow path through Africa and with a stick hit the dry leaves on the bushes, sending big flies buzzing upward. In a bare clearing we sat down.

"Have you any provisions?" she asked. But of course I had nothing. "Then we must first get some provisions," she decided, and we walked down another path until we came to some houses. "In that store over there," said Ingrid, "they don't sell licorice loose, only in rolls. You must ask, 'Do you sell licorice loose?' "

"Why?" I asked, "if you already know they don't?"

"I'm not going to tell you," she said. "Otherwise you'll be scared to ask."

"I'm not scared to ask," I said. "If I do, will I be your friend?" She nodded.

We entered the store and when the bell clanged, a fat woman in a shiny black coat appeared. "Do you sell licorice loose, please?" I asked. But she didn't.

Outside, Ingrid broke into a run. When we rounded the corner, she stopped and said, "Look," and she cautiously opened one hand a little for me to see. She had a fistful of currants, which she carefully let slide into the pocket of her dress.

"Now I am your friend," I said, and I took my friend Ingrid by the hand and went back to Africa. We ate the currants on the yellow hill, from which we could see the whole of Africa right up to the houses.

My friend Ingrid said nothing further but started looking at me. She moved her head very gently, so that her hair drifted slightly back and forth over her arms. It was as if her eyes were not moving. As I gazed back at her, I pointed to the right and said, "Those flowers over there, they're lady's-smock." But my friend remained silent, looking at me.

Then we both heard a bell from far away. She stood up and so did I. "That's the bell of our house," she said, and then, "I don't mind if I go steady with you." With her mouth wide open, my friend Ingrid kissed me very quickly, so that my mouth became wet and I could feel her teeth. Then she ran away fast. I did not leave until some time later, but I could easily find the way because she had pulled the leaves from the bushes and hedges all along the gardens.

At my uncle Alexander's house a piece of paper had been spiked onto the gate. I unfolded it and read, "Your uncle is a queer." At that moment my uncle Alexander came down the garden path and I crumpled the note into my pocket. "Where have you been?" he asked.

"To Africa, Uncle," I said, "with my friend Ingrid."

"It's time for your train," he said. "Here's your suitcase." And he disappeared into the garden.

It was in the same season, but six years later, when I next went to see my uncle Antonin Alexander, this time to stay. I was able to reach the bell now, but because I thought he would probably be sitting on the terrace, I went to the back of the house. First I saw his hands.

"Is that you, Philip?" he asked.

"Yes, Uncle."

"Have you brought me anything?"

I handed him the rhododendrons I had cut from the garden next to his.

"I appreciate it very much," he said. And without getting up, because he had grown even older, he made a small bow so that his head briefly came into the light. "Sit down," he said. There was no chair, and so I sat at his feet on the wooden steps leading to the garden, with my back toward him. "That boy who said you had girl's hair was right," the voice behind me began. "The fact that he said it was a defense; you must remember that. People have to defend themselves against the unfamiliar." He paused, and the garden and the evening stirred around us.

"There is an old story about paradise lost. We all know it well, which is not surprising, for the only real purpose of our existence is to try to regain that paradise, although it is impossible for us to do so." He breathed heavily. "We can get close to it, though, Philip, closer than people think. But as soon as someone approaches this no-longer-existing paradise, people start defending themselves against him, for the strange thing is that people's eyes see the wrong way. Their lenses have been cut crookedly, for the nearer I get to that impossible, perfect state, the smaller I become. Yet as I grow smaller, I grow bigger in others' eyes, which is something they have to defend themselves against, for people always draw the wrong conclusions.

"When I wear rings"—and he raised his hands to show the rings, which I now knew to be made of brass and glass—"they say it is vanity and that I have given in to my vanity.

But there is no such thing as giving in to vanity; there is only renunciation of vanity, and that means decay. I decay because I make a sacrifice to my vanity, and therefore I become smaller. To them I become strange, and therefore bigger; but to myself I become ever more ordinary, and therefore smaller. It is the same with islands. The smaller the island, the greater its exclusiveness, but the smallest island is almost sea. And it is not the people around us that are the sea, but the god we want to become, whom we see before us, and who bears our name—that god is the sea. We always live close to our own divinity. You mustn't forget that. Do you understand what I mean?"

"Not altogether, Uncle," I said.

"I am very tired," he said, and continued, but now very slowly. "We are born to become gods and to die, and that is crazy. The latter, the fact that we have to die, is terrible only for us because it means we can never attain the first, which is to become gods. But the former is terrible for the others. A god is something dreadful, because a god is perfect. And man fears nothing as much as perfection and strangeness. The strangeness is a reflection of divinity, which is an endless scale of possibilities, including the strangest. Yet we always get stuck somewhere along the way, and it is hard to have to admit it." He stopped because he was unable to say any more, but a moment later he said very clearly, "And then there is such a thing as ecstasy. Do you understand," he asked, "what I just said?"

I don't think I do, I thought, and I said, "A bit."

He took the flowers from his lap and stood up. "Come," he said, "we're going to have a celebration." I lay down on my sofa and he on his. "Oh, dammit," I heard him say. "You are so mortal, you, but you must never stop. Promise me you must never stop being crazy and trying to become a god." I heard him laugh and then sing softly:

> Où allez vous?
> Au Paradis!
> Si vous allez au Paradis je vais aussi.

"Say that to me," he called. "Go on, say it." And I sang, "Où allez vous?" and he responded urgently, "Au Paradis." I replied, "Si vous allez au Paradis je vais aussi."

Then my uncle Alexander fetched the little suitcase and we took the bus to Loenen and from there to Loosdrecht. The lowland was peaceful as always under the evening sky, and when we had spread out the canvas on the grass, we drank some of the Courvoisier and spoke no more.

Later, when it was night, we walked to the bus stop on the dike. This time there was no girl in a red coat. Inside the bus, my uncle came to sit beside me and he said, "She wasn't there this time, that girl who kissed that boy on the mouth; but to us I think she was still there, for the things that surround us remain filled with our memories. All the same, a mouth isn't the most important—hands are. It's the hands that are the most beautiful."

In the street, after we had gotten off the bus, he said, "Tonight I will play for you." When we arrived home and he sat down at the harpsichord, it was as though he were no longer tired. "Partita number two," he announced—"symphony"—and as he huddled above the keys like a large frayed bird, he whispered, "Grave adagio." I lay on my sofa with my face turned toward him, listening to the small, wistful sound of the keys against the strings and to my uncle Alexander's sniffing. "Allemande," he said, "allemande, courante, saraband—can you see them dancing—beautiful, beautiful." Suddenly the thought struck me that there was no one I loved so much as my uncle Antonin Alexander, as I watched him play the rondeau. He turned his head with the wide green eyes toward me for a moment and whispered, "Vivace, do you see? Oh."

After the last movement, the tumultuous caprice, he remained seated with his arms hanging down. "I ought to go on playing, but I can't," he said. Presently he stood up, and I also rose. His eyes sparkled again and were deep as water when he said, "This is Mr. Bach, Johann Sebastian Bach." I bowed and pretended to shake hands. "And this is Vivaldi." My uncle pointed around the room. "Antonio Vivaldi, Domenico Scarlatti." And he called out other names—"Geminiani, Bonporti, Corelli"—and I bowed and said, "Sono tanto felice . . . Philip, Philip Emmanuel Vanderley. I am honored. It is a pleasure."

When I had shaken hands with all of them, I asked if I could go to bed. "Yes," said my uncle Alexander, "you must go to bed. It has grown late because they all came. You'd better go upstairs now. It is the fourth door along the landing."

The room was exactly the same, and when I woke up in the morning I saw the books again, exactly as I had left them, and also the rhododendrons beside my bed. I wondered what it had been like when my uncle Alexander looked in on me during the night, and I reflected that the boy in the portrait on the wall was there as well, watching me all night. I thought he had become even more handsome. And suddenly it was as if he said to me, "I have a secret." I looked at him again, but he had grown indifferent once more, and distant—and yet it was as if he had just run his hands through his hair.

I opened the lid of the record player and took the handle out of the box. Then I wound it up, and when I had lowered the needle onto the record, I went to the door to listen for my uncle Alexander. His rapid footsteps could be heard above the off-key wailing of the tenor and the hateful click of the scratch. He threw the door open. His face was blotched and red, and I could see that his palms were sweaty. His mouth hung open and there was spittle in the corners. Yet he did not shout, and when I had stopped the record, he said, "I will tell you everything." The boy on the wall seemed to move his lips, but that may have been my imagination. We went downstairs into the garden and sat on a bench with our feet in the tall, wet grass.

"He was called Paul Sweeloo," my uncle began, "and he was here with his father on long leave from the Dutch East Indies. His mother was from the Indies, but she was dead, I believe. She wasn't there at any rate, and Paul never talked about her. He lived in this house, but the garden was much bigger then and bordered on mine, which was where those new houses are now. I often saw him walking here, and as he thought no one was about, he always talked aloud to himself. I couldn't hear what he said because he didn't come close enough to the fence. I did notice, though, that he never laughed and that he always pulled things to pieces with his hands or tore off leaves. I never dared call out to him, but once he came so close to my garden that I could hear what he said. 'There is no one,' he said, 'no one at all.'"

My uncle shifted about on the seat and moved his feet back and forth through the grass, making it rustle. "Yes," he said "and maybe it is because I said something then that I now sit here on this bench, for I said, 'That's not true, I am here.' The boy turned around and I saw he had the eyes of an animal, a beast of prey. They were black eyes, and when they found me in my garden, they would not leave me again. He twitched his mouth and shook his head wildly. 'Who are you?' he said, and came closer, 'I don't know you.' 'I live in the house next door,' I replied, and climbed over the fence.

"He helped me get down, for I wasn't very good at climbing fences. 'You're quite an old man,' he said. 'Your hair is already a bit gray. Why are you talking to me?' 'You shouldn't go about on bare feet,' I said. 'The grass is much too wet.' 'Who cares! Look,' and he showed me the callouses under his feet. 'In Indonesia I always go barefoot.' And suddenly he stamped his foot on the ground. 'You must get out of my garden—you're an old man.'

"It is more than forty years ago now, but he was ten at the time, so I was much older than he. 'Help me get over the fence then,' I said. 'No,' he said. 'You can easily get over it by yourself.' But it was a high fence and I was afraid I would fall and that he would laugh at me, and so I said, 'I have something the matter with my leg.'

"He came up to help me and I felt how strong he was when he locked his hands to give me a leg up. 'My shoes will make your hands dirty.' 'Take them off then,' he said impatiently, 'or are you scared of getting your feet wet?' It wasn't that, but I thought my feet would look ridiculously old and white beside his. 'Don't bother,' I said. 'I'll manage by myself.' Of course I fell, on my side of the fence, but when I looked up to see if he was laughing, he had gone. 'Hey, I called. 'Come out, you, I can see you. I'm staying here until you come out. I'll stay here for as long as I have to.' "

"Yes," said my uncle Alexander, "so I stayed there and thought how ridiculous I must appear to him, who sat spying on me somewhere in the bushes like a hunter. My pants were torn and it had started to rain softly, so I began to feel cold and wet. Suddenly the wind got up as well, and the tree I was standing under shook its drops all over me. But the trees in his garden didn't move, and when I looked around I saw that the other trees in my own garden were also quite still under the soft, shroudlike rain, and then he burst out laughing right above my head and shook the branches even harder. 'Come down,' I called. 'You'll fall any minute.' 'I never fall,' he called back, and let himself slide down like some lithe animal. 'You have to go in for your dinner,' he said. 'I heard a gong in your house.' I asked him, 'Will you come and have dinner with me?' and I thought he would say no; but he said, 'I don't mind,' and we went to my house to eat.

"During dinner he said nothing, and I wasn't quite sure what to say to him either. Halfway through the meal he suddenly stood up and said, 'Now I have to go to my house for dinner. Bye.' He left the room and pulled the door shut behind him. The next day I was sitting near his garden in my summerhouse, but I didn't see him; nor did I see him in the days that followed. I thought he might have gone back to the Indies, but a week later he was suddenly there again. I was sitting in my summerhouse when I heard him call. 'Coo-ee,' he called, and he made his voice rise the way children do when they call out to one another. 'Coo-ee, Coo-ee, where are you?'

"His appearance was a surprise, for he was wearing gleamingly polished boots, long black socks, and a stiff new sailor suit. 'Why are you all dressed up?' I asked. He shrugged his shoulders. 'I wanted it to be my birthday today.' 'Is it your birthday?' 'No, of course not, stupid. I said I *wanted* it to be my birthday. You have to come, too, this afternoon, and you must bring lots of people. My dad isn't at home, and I want you to come and all those other people, too, because on birthdays there are always lots of guests and they all bring presents.' 'Who should I bring?' I asked him. 'Your friends, of course. You have friends, haven't you? So they can all come even if they're just as old as you.' 'But I don't have any friends'—I was becoming exasperated. 'Liar,' he said, stamping his foot furiously. He looked very beautiful just then, with his eyes opened big and wide. 'You're a liar; you *must* have friends.'"

My uncle Alexander sighed. "It was very difficult," he said. "I told him I might have a few friends but that they would certainly not be able to come on an ordinary weekday. You should have seen him. He became more and more beautiful in his anger and shouted, 'Then I'll get a present just from you.' 'No, of course not,' I said quickly. 'My friends will give me something for you if they can't come themselves.' He tilted his head to one side and pressed his lips. 'Honestly?' he asked. 'What will they give me then? I'd like them to give me books, and it should say on the title page that they're for me alone.' 'What kinds of books?' I asked. But he shrugged his shoulders. 'It doesn't matter'—he reflected a moment—'I'd like big ones best or, er . . . German ones.' 'Can you read German then?' I asked. 'Oh, drop dead,' he said, and went home. On the way he turned once more and called, 'At half-past three!' 'Half-past three!' I called back.

"In the afternoon he was no longer wearing his sailor suit. 'It hurts my neck and it itches everywhere. And you're the only one here, anyway. What's in that suitcase?' 'The presents my friends have sent.' 'Are there lots? It's a big suitcase, but of course it's not full.' I opened the lock with a click; the suitcase was full of books—the books you saw upstairs. He ran his hands over them. 'All of them,' he whispered, 'all of them.' He swayed back and forth on his feet and asked me, 'All of them?'

"He started taking them out and putting them in a row. 'Who gave me all these?' he asked. I invented friends I did not have and said they were all very sorry they were unable to come in person. Meanwhile, he counted the books. 'Jesus,' he said, 'there are so many. But there are seven all the same here, these German ones.' 'They're French,' I said, 'and they are not quite the same. They're different volumes of one book.' 'Really?' he asked."

My uncle Alexander looked at me as if he expected me to say something. But I wouldn't because I feared that he would then tell me nothing about the record player. So there was silence until finally he said, "That is all."

"And the record player?" I asked.

"No," said my uncle.

After a long silence he continued. "That afternoon we celebrated his birthday. I sat in a chair by the window while he added up the pages of all his books. I was not allowed to help him because he thought I might make a mistake and then he wouldn't know for sure. So I watched him. I think he had forgotten me, for he bit his lip with his upper teeth, and from time to time he grunted softly and kicked with his feet against the table.

"A month later the house was up for sale. They were going back to the Indies, his father and he. I bought it, and when he had gone, I found the books together with the other things in the room."

"And the record player?" I asked.

"No," said my uncle Alexander.

"And he?"

"I don't know," said my uncle Alexander, and he stood up and went into the house. He shut the terrace doors behind him.

I stayed with my uncle Alexander for two years, and I learned a great deal from him because he was so old. And then, after two years, one evening in May I asked him if he would allow me to leave to go to France.

The evening before I was due to leave I suddenly saw that the harpsichord had disappeared. "Where's the harpsichord?" I asked. My uncle Antonin Alexander stood at the spot where it had been.

"Sometimes I am very tired after playing," he said. "Very tired, and I am old now. You will be gone for a long time, and maybe I still want to be here when you come back. Good night."

The next morning I found purple rhododendrons by my bed and a hundred-guilder note. When I walked through the living room on my way to catch the first train to Breda, I saw my uncle Alexander asleep on the sofa with his mouth half-open and his knees drawn up—and I saw his hands making movements on the floor.

Outside it was cold, and the house stood tall and ugly in the heavy mist. I did not walk past the houses that had been built on top of Africa.

2

Well, yes, hitchhiking! It wasn't so simple to get to Provence. There was, for instance, that man in the old Skoda, before Antwerp.

"How many cows are there in that field?" he asked.

"I don't know," I replied, "I can't count them that fast."

"Thirty-six!" he called out triumphantly. "Light me this cigarette, will you."

I put the cigarette between his gray lips and gave him a light. He inhaled deeply and blew the greasy smoke against the windshield and into my face. "Smoke screen. Haha!" he said. "But those cows, that's easy." He clicked his fingers, not very successfully because they were too chubby. "Very easy. You count the legs and divide by four." He looked at me to see if I'd laughed, so I did.

"Haha!" he roared. "You didn't know that one, did you! Good joke, that, a really hoary one. You've got lovely long hair, you—I say, I bet you play with little boys sometimes, don't you." He started pinching my leg gently.

"I want to get out," I said.

He braked so hard that I hit my head against the windshield. "Out," he said. "Piss off. And quick."

I grabbed my rucksack from the backseat, but it caught on something and the man punched it out of the car so that it fell against me. I ran and didn't stop till I heard him slam the door. He yelled through the window, "Sissy! Sissy!" before driving off.

I think I was trembling violently, but I could not go back, and so I started thumbing lifts again. Don't ask me how many days later I danced with a girl called Jacqueline, whose other name I do not know, at the Place du Forum in Arles. Her name must have been Jacqueline because the boys and girls that were dancing around us called out "Bonsoir, Jacqueline," and she called back "Bonsoir, Ninette, bonsoir, Nicole," and then she smiled at me and we danced on. Her hair moved with the dance, red and loose. We danced uninterruptedly with each other, and later in the evening she came closer to me and held her hands on my back and my neck.

"Are you leaving tomorrow, Philip?" she asked.

"Yes."

"Then you're going to take a long trip?"

"I don't know."

Most people had gone by now, and with a few other couples we danced by the big statue of Mistral to the music of an accordion. The music was sad, for Arles—on other nights silent and withdrawn in its many memories—was in somber league with the melody, and together, with their nostalgia and wistfulness, they closed in upon us, small group of dancers under the streetlights.

"You mustn't kiss me when you take me home," she said. "Promise you won't?"

"All right," I said, "I won't kiss you."

"And you mustn't look at the name of the street either," she whispered, "nor at the number. I don't want you to forget me, but you mustn't write to me. We are only passersby in a busy street, and you must never come back, because you don't bring luck."

"Why not?" I asked.

"It's what I think," she replied. "You were born old"—she ran her fingers over my lips—"you will never experience anything but memories, you will never meet anyone except to say goodbye, and you won't live a single day without thinking of the evening or the night."

We broke the circle of people and music, and I walked through streets in which I had not been before, and because she had asked me, I did not look at the name of the street in which she stopped. She drew me close to her and said, "Now you must go away. I won't turn around, because I want to see you walk out of the street." She put her hands on my face as if she hoped its shape would remain in her hands and ensure she would not forget and then she gently pushed me away until I was at arm's length from her.

"Turn around," she said. "You must go now." Her face in the yellow light of the streetlamp in front of her house became forlorn. "Turn," she said, "turn," and as I did, I still saw her hair gently moving with the wind. I slowly started following my strange, narrow shadow along the houses, through the streets, to the Promenade des Lices. From there I went to the Avenue des Alyscamps, which slopes down toward the old Roman cemetery. There are cypresses there, proud and mysterious, and the moon shone dangerously and bluishly on the graves. I leaned against a tomb and felt the chill of the stone penetrate my body, and suddenly I heard a disconcerting old voice speaking behind me:

> Dans Arles, ou sont les Alyscamps,
> quand l'ombre est rouge, sous les roses
> et clair le temps
>
> prends garde à la douceur des choses
> lorsque tu sens battre sans cause
> ton coeur trop lourd
>
> et que se taisent les colombes
> parle tout bas, si c'est d'amour
> au bord des tombes.

It was the voice of a man, and he spoke with the accent of Provence, with the heavy *r* and the dark stresses of southern countries. I did not turn around to look at him, but he took me by the arm and pulled me gently away. "As tu peur des pieux mystères passe plus loin du cimetière," he whispered. "Come. You must come with me. I have a story to tell you." He was old, but maybe it only seemed like that because he was so fat. His small evasive eyes lay deep under his rough gray eyebrows, which were pressed down by a layer of fat on the lower part of his forehead. His whole face was shapeless and sagging, and the hand that held my arm was as soft as a sponge. In the wide sleeves of a dirty black habit, his hairless arms appeared white and feminine.

"I know," he said. "I am fat. They say I am the fattest man in Provence, but I have to tell you a story. I saw you this evening in the Place du Forum, and yesterday in the church of Saint Trophyme. I kept my eye on you and I followed you."

Now I followed him, and because I did not know what to say, I said nothing as we walked back under the poplars and the cypresses. He breathed hard from the effort, and I held his arm as long as the road climbed. In front of my hotel he stopped.

"Get your baggage," he said. "Then we'll go."

"Where to?" I asked, but he looked at me in surprise and said, "To the story of course." And so I went with him.

In his old car we drove through a dead, ominous land that night. The moon rose regally from the extinguished, reddish earth. Strands of mist ran through the valleys, surrounding us like a danger from which we escaped again and again amid hard, sharp shrubs that looked like flocks of long-dead beasts climbing the hillsides toward the weirdly shaped rocks that bloomed in the nocturnal light. Occasionally we struck a wave of tepid warmth that, pressed down by the comfortless afternoon heat, slowly fanned out in the night, sometimes carrying with it the spicy scent of thyme and lavender.

Silently we drove on through Provence, where all the towns and villages resembled the abandoned mountain town of Les Baux—dead towns in which, by some ghostlike chance, the streetlights still burned and a clock sometimes struck by mistake. I fell asleep and woke only when the car stopped. We looked down. "There is the valley," he said, "and that is the village."

Now there was the first light of the sun. The houses lay far and insignificantly beneath us, huddled around the church like animals herded together. Amid the stony, infertile hillsides that would soon be pounded mercilessly by the sun, the village seemed like an entrancing breath of life near an almost dried-up river that ran through the middle of the valley.

"You get out here," he said. "My name is Maventer. *Ma* stands for magnus, big, and *venter* means belly. It isn't my real name, but everybody calls me that."

"Are you a monk?" I asked, but he said "No, I am not a monk," and then the man Maventer put my rucksack on the ground and turned the car around.

"And the story?" I asked

"You must go to the village," he said. "There is only one hotel, Chez Sylvestre. I shall be there later this week, but you mustn't mention me."

"All right," I said. "I shan't mention you."

I took my rucksack and started walking down the hill. He started away and called, "In about three days, I think, or maybe two," but I walked on. The rosy dust on the road billowed around my feet like a miniature sirocco and crept into my shoes and socks. Farther down, the rock-thyme flowered red and violet, the scrub became greener, and at last there was the village, almost friendly, with white and pink houses built seemingly without any plan, and gardens shaded by pine trees and cypresses.

It was not difficult to find the hotel Chez Sylvestre. The patronne was closing the shutters so that the sunlight would not beat its way in. I spoke to her and followed her indoors. "Un Hollandais," she said to the patron, and two men standing by the bar turned to look at me. It must be a small village, I thought, where hardly any strangers come; and it suddenly occurred to me that I did not know the name of the village. The men talked to each other in Provençal, and I could not understand them. The floor and the stairs were paved with hexagonal red tiles, and on the sparklingly whitewashed walls hung the same advertising posters as everywhere else—Cognac Hennessy, Noilly Prat, Saint Raphaël, Quinquina.

The boss, Sylvestre, showed me to my room at the front of

the building. I would be able to look out over the square with its old fountain and stone seats in the shade of many trees, but he immediately closed the shutters.

"The sun is terrible here," he said, and I replied, "As usual."

"In the summer, yes," he nodded. "I'll bring you some water."

A moment later he returned with a large glass of pastis, as they drink it only here, and a bucket of water, which he put under the wooden washstand after pouring some into the pitcher. "Everything all right?" he asked.

"Très bien," I said, "merci," and he laughed and left the room. I lay down on the huge bed and laughed because it creaked when I moved and because the sheets were made of coarse cotton and smelled like children who have been swimming in the river.

When I woke up, it was late in the afternoon and someone had put bread and wine beside me, covered with a serviette. Looking out the window I realized why some of the houses were built like fortresses. Toward evening the heat becomes unbearable and grandiose in its ruthlessness, so that man and beast seek the dark and half-dark corners of their homes and wait there till night falls. The village, therefore, was dead when I went outside.

I slowly walked across the square to drink some lukewarm water from the fountain, and because I did not see any of the living, I visited the dead. The tombs stood haphazardly around a large, rough wooden cross, like the houses of the living around the church. The dead lay peacefully enclosed within a hedge of maythorn and hornbeam.

Later, when I got to know the living, I discovered that they did not differ so very much from the dead; they too belonged to one another in their somber taciturnity. The bitterness of the red soil, hard to till and full of painful stones, had pervaded their bodies, together with that whispering melancholy that roams around in the evening when the heat has reluctantly retreated from the village. Then, the metallic click-

click of the jeu de boules is almost the only sound to be heard, apart from the glasses at Sylvestre's, the animals, the evening breeze in the cypresses, and the hesitant singing of children.

> Alix ma bonne amie
> Il est temp de quitter
> le monde et ses intrigues
> avec ses vanités.

I remember their song, for in the evenings I sat by my window at Sylvestre's watching the men and the children. They neither saw nor knew me, but I learned their names, and after two days I knew who was best at the jeu de boules and who drank the most. The children played by the fountain, but strangely and almost soundlessly, like children that have been told to be quiet because someone is ill. Both men and children played, while in the falling darkness women came with pails and pitchers to fetch water. I could easily see it all from my window, between the heavy, bending branches of the wisteria that breathed like a big live animal, mysteriously moved by the hands of a small breeze. Facing me there was always the church, and I knew it was crumbling within and that on the altar lay a dusty cloth of red velvet embroidered in gold letters—*Magister adest et vocat te,* the Master is here and calls thee. Church and churchyard were permeated with the life of this village, in which the names always remained the same—those of the living in the café or by the well, and those of the dead under the large faded portraits on their graves. Those enameled and cardboard portraits were locked behind dirty glass, together with strands of dull hair, pale artificial flowers, and faded ribbons. Covered in dust and cobwebs, the pictures were set in round frames of thin, flattened, heavily curled iron. When I first saw them, it seemed to me as though an old, somber superstition lived among these people and ruled over their graves; for behind the rigidity of those portraits I soon began to recognize the faces of the living whom I had seen from my window, talking and drinking.

In the afternoon hours, when the sun established its dominion over the lifeless houses, I moved among the dead Peyeroux, the dead Rapets, the dead Ventours. Flowers I had picked early in the morning and kept in water in my room, I put on the graves of children, though I don't know why, except that perhaps it gave me pleasure. The evening before the man Maventer came, the priest waited for me. He was sitting on the family grave of the Peyeroux. "I think they'll forgive me," he said. "We were good friends, and in any case I shall soon be here myself, over there in that corner. That seems a pleasant enough spot, don't you think? The sun can't reach there quite so easily, and if, who knows, a stranger were to put flowers there, they might stay fresh a little longer."

At home in the presbytère he poured two tall glasses of wine, like Sylvestre, right up to the brim. "I don't suppose you have read our Mistral," he said, "but he sang of this wine in 'Mireille.'"

> Alor, en terro de Prouvenço
> I' a mai que mai divertissenço
> Lou bon Muscat de Baume e lou Frigolet
> Alor. . .

"Muscat de Baume!" He laughed and tapped his glass against mine. "I saw how you made acquaintance with the dead," he said. "It's the best way. Sometimes the dead are more forthcoming than the living; and as to that, the living aren't very forthcoming here."

"I know," I said, "but I like them."

"Maybe," he hesitated, "maybe, but life is hard and grim here, and sometimes hostile like the soil, which yields a few tomatoes and melons and some meager grain only after many caresses. It can be as bitter as the grass that the sheep and goats live on in the plain before they go up into the mountains in the spring. Life here is a life of necessity. There is God, a few other people, and the soil, and each of these is as hard as the other.

"I know," he said, "and I am in a position to know. Over

there''—he opened the shutters of the window overlooking the street and pointed to the hillsides, which glittered so fiercely that I had to shield my eyes—''are my tomatoes and my melons and sometimes, if they don't die, my flowers for the church, carnations. And that isn't all. There is the winter, which is harsher here than in the North and which can strike like the sun; and *mon vieux,* then there is also the mistral.

''Do you know the mistral?'' he asked. I had never heard of it, or perhaps I had but did not remember it. He told me about this wind, which scourges the valleys and the people alike with its coldness while the sun continues to shine impassively, a wind that knows where to find people no matter where they are hiding. It finds its way into every shelter and behind every closed door, ''and sometimes strange things happen here then,'' he said, ''for it fatigues the mind most of all, to the breaking point. A trivial quarrel strikes like lightning, and leaps and rages like flames in hay. We all know it, the living here and the dead there.'' He nodded toward the cemetery behind the hawthorn.

''One day, when the mistral had been blowing through the village for a week, as cruelly as a man seeking revenge, Claude Peyeroux beat his wife to death and hanged himself. And the mistral also blew when this Maventer first set foot here. Later he went to live at the castle. And it was once again on a day when the mistral blew that the marchioness Marcelle left.''

''Who is Maventer?'' I asked.

''His name isn't really Maventer. Some latter-day rhetorician invented that. I don't know his real name. He used to be a choir monk with the Benedictines. Are you a Catholic?''

''No,'' I said, ''but I know about them, about the Benedictines.''

''Good,'' he said, ''but this Maventer was one of the last choir monks who was not a priest. There are lay brothers who work on the land and who look after the house and the clothing, and then there are monks who sing prayers and have other functions in the monastery, such as bookkeeper or supervisor of the novices or whatever. In the old days you could be in the choir without being ordained. That was what was called a choir monk, but this is now very rare. In any case, Maventer left, and that is to me no reason to condemn him, for he had entered the order too young, and, it is said, under a certain pressure from his family. It is difficult to talk about someone about whom you know a great deal and yet very little, because in the end"—he looked at me as he readjusted the biretta on his thin white hair—"in the end we know very little about one another.

"He used to be a wanderer. He was a welcome guest at every party, and his name was known for miles around. He and his accordion. He was at the cherry picking in Cavaillon and Carpentras and at the grape picking in the Durance Valley and always in the same worn habit that he still wears, God knows why. But all that ended three years ago when he came to live here at Experi, not very far away. He is no longer welcome at weddings and in the houses of the leading families and the clergy, where he used to be held in high esteem for his knowledge. He knows more about Thomas Aquinas than I have ever known, and at all the contests in Arles and even in Avignon he would beat everyone with his knowledge of the classical poets and the old Provençal troubadours. They say he knows all Horace's odes and epodes by heart, and it may well be true.

"I often saw him at night, him and the little marchioness—yes, they were a fitting pair, for she was a strange girl. Sometimes they would walk down the street here at night. She was very slim and small, and she wore tight pants such as they say are worn by the women in Paris, and small low-heeled shoes. She would walk quickly across the square, almost without a sound. I would be standing behind my window in the dark, because since I have grown old, I have become a very light sleeper.

"They came from the direction of Experi—that is the name of the castle. He'd be walking some ten paces behind her, heavy and rather ominous because of his huge shadow, and panting because he walked fast, but she never took any notice of him and walked with her head down, talking to herself. Sometimes she came alone; then she would walk slower and drink from the fountain, and sometimes there would be flowers in the churchyard the next morning.

Once I spoke to her. She was alone that night, drinking at the fountain. 'Mademoiselle,' I said, 'would you like to drink some of my wine?' I fetched the wine I always had ready at night, and we sat on the steps in front of the presbytère. But she said nothing, and when I asked her whether she wasn't afraid, all alone in the night, she said, 'Of course not.' And then she looked at me with that oriental face of hers, which I have never been able to understand properly as I understand the faces of the people here, grown and shaped like my own. Her face was withdrawn and enigmatic, and she whispered, 'I am making a story.' 'Yes,' I said, 'I know you are making a story.' And, 'I don't want to interfere with it, because it is your story, but please make sure it is a good one.' She only nodded."

He was silent. "Did she have an oriental face?" I asked.

"Her mother came from Laos, but she died. The father was an officer in the foreign legion, and he was hardly ever here. He was killed in Indochina. Then there is an aunt, but we never see her here, and the servants, and then of course Maventer. People talk a lot, but nobody really knows anything. They've been talking ever since I've been here, but none of us has ever been inside the castle."

That evening in my room I expected Maventer, for the furniture did not hide behind the approaching night as it had done the other evenings; it continued, big and disquietingly self-confident, to surround me, to tell me that this was the last time it was part of me. And also the smells that lived in the room, of aging wood, of sheets washed in the stream with hard country soap, were stronger and more independent than before, certain of their victory over the strange, now almost vanished smell of my body and my clothes.

And just as a man who always sleeps by the sound of a clock

wakes when the clock stops ticking, so I slowly went to my window to see the man Maventer arrive when the clicking of the boules game suddenly stopped. "Dutchman!" he called from outside. "Dutchman, come out. I have a story I want to tell you."

We walked for a long time on a road skirting the hillside and later on a steeply climbing path. Here and there the night suddenly appeared in the scrub or between the big rocks. It accompanied us until we were so high up that we could see the purple chain of the Alpes de Provence and the mountain ranges of Luberon and Ventoux in a wide circle around us. Before the night had touched and hidden everything, Maventer pointed out the jewels in the chain—the Vaucluse mountains, la montagne de Lure, la montagne de Chabre.

The castle, or whatever it was, stood mighty and alive against the mountain. Maventer took me to a field with the same scratchy ground as everywhere else. You would have thought that its black stones did not belong there but rather on the moon or in some other place where there is no life, and that someone had put them there according to a preplanned pattern, with a big black rock, like a burnt piece of coal fallen from a giant fireplace, in the center. We sat down on it.

"This is the animal graveyard," said Maventer. "This is where it all began. I sat here and she came up to me. 'You are Maventer,' she said. 'I am.' 'Can you read English?' 'Yes.' 'And write it?' When I said I could, she sat down on the ground in front of me, where you are now. 'You'll get dirty,' I said. 'Why don't you sit on a rock?' But she didn't seem to hear me. She drew a circle around herself with the heel of an outstretched foot. 'I'm in the circle,' she said. 'You are not in the circle. Now you must put your foot inside it, because I have to ask you a question.'

"I moved so that my feet were in the circle, too, and she sprinkled fine sand over them. 'Don't do that,' I said. 'You're making everything dirty.' 'I want you to write a letter in English.' 'Who to?' I asked. 'To this person.' She pulled her jacket toward herself and took out a *Saturday Evening Post.*

She opened it and pointed to a photograph of a ballet dancer. 'I want you to write to her and ask her if she will come and live here.' 'No,' I said. She looked through me and blew the hair from her forehead. 'Why not?' she asked. 'Because she won't come anyway.'"

Maventer looked at me and said, "If I had known her then the way I know her now, I would never have made a mistake like that, but I didn't know her yet, so I said 'because she won't come anyway.' And she merely smiled—not even at me, no—she smiled to herself and to some invisible persons or things that were always with her, and she told me I was stupid 'because,' she said, 'of course she won't come, but how can I pretend she will if you don't first write a letter in English inviting her.'"

"Do you understand that?" he asked me. I understood it perfectly and said, "I think so."

"That's how it always was. She pretended; she was so unusual." The voice beside me went on and on, but I saw her and suddenly I was sure that this was no longer the real world, for things were alive and self-possessed in another, different reality that all at once became perceptible, visible. It touched me and detached me until I floated on the voice of Maventer, who walked among the stones in the animal graveyard, where she sat drawing in the dust and hearing—perhaps, I don't know—herself say in his voice, in the story he was telling, "Maventer, when will you be going to town again?" and his response, "Why?"

He asked, "Are you listening?"

"Yes, I'm listening," I said.

"We went to the bank once every three months, and she was always interested only in the adding machines. 'I want to add myself up,' she said, and the next time we went to the bank in town, she asked at the counter if she could have a go on one of those machines. They said all right, and from her glove she took a piece of paper with figures written on it, which she tapped out on the machine. She pressed the addition key and pulled the lever.

"For a few days after that I did not see her, which was nothing unusual, as it happened quite often that she stayed in her own part of the castle and didn't show herself anywhere. On this occasion it was a long time before I saw her again. She came to see me in the library. 'Maventer,' she said, 'I'm back.' She came to stand near me. 'I've been away.' I had been there long enough to know I must not say that she had not been away at all but had stayed in her own rooms She went on: 'Do you remember that piece of paper?' 'Yes,' I said, 'yes, on which you added yourself up.' She nodded. 'That evening,' she whispered, and she came closer to me as if we were conspirators, 'that evening I put the piece of paper outside because it was windy. Then I went to my room to see if it would happen, what I wanted. And it did happen. I blew away.'

"When we went outside, she said, 'I've added myself up,' and she showed me the piece of paper. I can't recall all the figures; I only remember that one of them was 152. 'What's that?' I asked. 'That's my height, didn't you know?' she answered. 'Yes,' I said, 'it's your height, and what are you going to do now?' 'I'm not going to tell you, but you must shake hands with me because I am going away.' 'Where to?' I asked. But she shrugged her shoulders. She didn't know.

"'There was a breeze that night,' she continued. 'In my room upstairs, the scent of the honeysuckle was on my windowsill and remained with me even when I arrived in that country.' 'Which country?' 'Oh, it was a strange country to which the wind took the piece of paper I had added myself up on. When I arrived there, people came out to welcome me. Everywhere there was honeysuckle, and everything, everything, smelled of it. But the people were sad, and I asked the man who was showing me around, "Why are people here so sad?" "It's true," he said. "They are very sad. I'll show you." And at night, when all the people were asleep, we walked through the town.

"'The man said, "This is a bookstore," but the display window was empty, or rather there was only one thin little book in it. There was no honeysuckle or any other kinds of flowers, and there were no flags either, as there were on the other stores and houses. "There's only one book there," I said. "Yes," he said, "you can look inside." We both looked with our foreheads pressed against the windowpane, and by the light of the streetlamp I saw that the shelves on which there should have been books were empty. I saw only one copy of that one little book, on a shelf at the back.

"'He said, "Now we'll go to the state library," and we walked through the streets until we came to it. The man opened the doors, and when we entered, it was as if our footsteps resounded not only on the marble floor but also against the walls and the ceiling and everywhere, louder and louder. "I think I'm afraid," I said, but he said it didn't matter, because he was with me. We walked through the different rooms, but there were no books anywhere, only empty shelves and big empty bookcases. Only, in a few places, that one little book was there.

"'I was really afraid, because the walls were high and white above the shelves and we heard only each other and our footsteps, and because there were no books. "Why aren't there any books?" I asked. "In a library there are supposed to be books, aren't there?" "Usually there are," he answered, "but you see, he is dead." Who is dead? I thought. "It was a boy," he went on, "a small boy whose hair was already going slightly gray, and he was always ill. He was the only one who was able to write, for in this country it isn't as in other countries. Some people here were able to have children, others could build houses, and still others made flags to display when there were visitors like you. But no one here could write poems or stories or a book. But this boy was always sick, and when he died he had finished only the first chapter. There it is." And he pointed at the little thin book.'

"She paused. After a while she said, 'Then I left that country because it was so sad there.'"

Maventer looked at me again. "Have you ever been in such a country?" he asked.

"No," I said, "but maybe I will go to one someday."

Then we were silent. I didn't want him to say any more, so that I might see what she was drawing in the sand.

"What are you drawing?" I asked.

"Plane trees," she said. "They're behind you." I looked around.

"What are you looking at?" asked Maventer.

"At those trees," I said. "What kind of trees are they?"

"They're plane trees," he replied.

"What are those letters you are drawing now?" I asked her.

"A *K*," she whispered, so I knew it was meant to be a secret. "A *K* and an *R*, a *U*, an *S*, an *A*, and another *A*."

"That isn't a word," I said. "K-R-U-S-A-A."

"I know," she said. "It's a silly word."

"What did you say?" asked Maventer.

"Nothing," I said, and he gave me a doubtful look.

"I thought you were saying something," he said.

"No, I didn't say anything."

He continued. "Not so long afterward she went away again. We had gone to Avignon by car, and as I had to see some people there, she would spend the time in the library. But when I collected her in the evening and asked her what she had been reading, she did not answer. It was odd; her hair was wet, and she sat in the back of the car and did not speak all through the journey. At Experi she went straight to her own rooms. She didn't come down again until two days later.

"I was sitting by the gate this time, and started when she touched me on the shoulder from behind. 'Maventer, I'm back. I've been very far away this time,' she said. It isn't true, I thought, and I said, 'But you didn't have a piece of paper. Where have you been?' 'Oh, it was different this time. I didn't know how I would manage to get away, but on the inner door of the reading room there is a notice saying that everyone who goes in there to read or study must sign the register on entering and on leaving. Well, I signed my name when I went in, but not when I left. So I was really still inside, even though the room was locked after the last people had gone.

"'It was raining when I arrived in that country, and as I wasn't really anywhere, I could travel as I pleased. It was raining, and it was evening. I was outside a station and got on a tram. Opposite me sat a man. "What are you looking at?" he asked. "At your hands." They moved against and over each other like fighting animals, those hands, ceaselessly. "Don't take any notice," said the man. "It is of no importance; it's always like that before I play. Would you like a free ticket?"

"'We got out on a wide, busy street. The man walked ahead of me through the crowds, and he turned his head and called out, "It's late. I must hurry." He ran on ahead of me while his hands kept moving about as if he were frightened and trying to ward off a threatening danger. I would have preferred to stay on the street because the lights floated on the asphalt as on the surface of a deep dark water. But because the man with the hands had given me that ticket, I entered the concert hall. I was the last person in the corridor and was barely allowed in before the doors were closed.

"'The hall was so strange! There were so many grand pianos, perhaps as many as a hundred, standing in a hazy orange light like mourners gathering for a funeral procession. The people sitting at them were talking to one another, the way they always do at concerts, filling the hall with suppressed murmurs. A lady showed me to my piano, fairly near the front. I didn't buy a program because I saw they were blank. At the back of the hall people started saying sh-h-h, and I looked at the platform to see if the man had arrived yet. And then I noticed that there was no piano on the platform, only a chair. We stood up and clapped when the man climbed up on the platform. His hands no longer moved, and he bowed to the audience, sat down, and waited until we stopped clapping.

"'Then we started playing. I was sure I knew the melody, which wandered gently and tenderly about the hall, just as if only one piano were playing; but I could not remember the names of either the piece or the composer. I couldn't even think what kind of music we were playing, nor even from which period. When it was finished, he stood up to thank us for the applause that now came storming up like thunder. Then he sat down on his chair again, his hands at rest as if they had never moved, and we played again. I was unfamiliar with the pieces, but it didn't matter, and it doesn't matter now. All I know is that it was an old, enchanting kind of music. He sat quietly on his chair on the platform, far away, and when we had finished playing, he got up and thanked us because we applauded him. And at the end of the evening we gave him such an ovation that we even played an encore.

"'Oh, Maventer,' she said, 'I wasn't at all glad to come back from that country. One day I will go away and not come back.' 'That's true,' I said. 'One day you'll go away and not come back.' She then asked, 'Will you drive me to The Country? It is still light.' The Country was about seven kilometers away from here. She had found it once, and it was hers, just as her part of the castle was hers, and some places in the dining room, the corridors, the garden, anywhere—places she went and that we all had to keep away from. At first it was difficult to remember all those places. 'Please, Maventer,' she would say, 'you're not supposed to walk through there.' She never said why. Maybe there were things there that she saw, but it doesn't really matter very much, I think.

"So that evening we drove to The Country. When we got out of the car, she said, 'I'm going away tomorrow, and I'm not coming back. I'm going to play something big this time.' She told me many things that evening, and frankly I can't remember all of them; but I do remember her as she sat there, for it was as though she had absorbed the independent, you might say the conscious, life of the trees and the other things in which she believed so strongly. She became the shadow and the quivering of the silver spruce that grew there and the aged, cracked crimson of the dried-up riverbed. I can't say it in any other way—she expanded and grew larger in order to encompass the evening, the scent of the bay tree, and finally the whole valley. That evening the valley was created afresh with the hands of a lunatic who had come into possession of the moon and who painted and struck the rocks and the trees with the light of the moon until an unbearable madness seized control of the landscape, and all things began to breathe and live together with her, unbearably.

"'You are afraid,' she said. 'Yes,' I replied, but she wasn't listening. 'You are afraid because your world, your safe world in which you were able to recognize things has gone, because you now see that things become created anew every moment and that they are alive. You people always think that your world is the real one, but it isn't; mine is. It is the life behind the first, visible reality—a life that is tangible and that trembles. And what you see, what people like you see, is dead. Dead.'"

Maventer sighed. "She lay down on her back, and I saw she was small and slender like a boy." He was silent.

"And then?" I asked.

"Well," he said, slowly letting his hands slide from his lap in a gesture of sorrow or helplessness, "I broke the spell. I walked away and waited farther down, by the car. And the next morning she went away, and she won't come back. As for me, I have decided to grow old. I am no longer young, and I have lived through much; but as long as she was there, I couldn't grow old. I simply couldn't. And now she has gone, and you have come in order to let me tell the story. It has been told, and now I can start growing old.

"I went to The Country one more time, and everything was ordinary—a riverbed of dry red mud, some rocks and trees—nothing to be afraid of. How odd now, to start growing old. After that, dying won't be far off. He rose. "Now you must leave. I'll take you to Digne in the car."

And so he did, and we said goodbye there, on the railroad crossing in a bend of the road to Grenoble, and he held my hand between the sponges of his hands. His eyes still avoided mine, and because I never saw properly what they were like, I never really knew him. After that bend in the road I could no longer see him, but I heard him turn the car around, and the sound grew weaker and died away.

Finally there was silence, and I thought I might perhaps find her, somewhere.

Book Two

1

"That isn't a house," I said as we turned into the drive, "and I don't even know your name."

"Fay," she said.

It was a ruin. Closer by, I could see it better in the tearful light with which the day had begun. Vile white-green grass, bracken, and all kinds of harsh flowers grew rank over the colorless heaps of stone. Rotted and mildewed window frames leaned in grotesque postures against frightened little pillars. Doors, on which dirty lichen vegetated among flakes of paint, stood disconsolately up to their knees in the dead, rust-colored water of a bomb crater, and exhausted from a desperate death struggle, disintegrating furniture and mattresses lay sprawling among the bushes, spreading a sickly smell of decay.

Half the turret had been knocked down, and you could look inside as if into a body on the dissecting table; a freestone winding staircase, slashed by bullets, gleamed bluishly. Fay preceded me up the stairs. Halfway, there was a low, clumsily hewn door, which she kicked open with her foot. "This is the only habitable room." she said. It was long and narrow. In the light of a lamp she lit, I saw here and there on the walls the remains of dark red leather wall hangings with runic patterns in faded gold. There were two windows, one of which was boarded up with planks and sheets of cardboard. These windows were to the left of the door; on the opposite wall hung a long, irregular row of about twenty photographs, mostly of men and boys, but there were also a few girls among them. Some of these portraits were very large, others were postcard size, and there were even some passport photographs. Over each of these faces a cross had been drawn in red ink, with mathematical accuracy. I didn't recognize any of them. Underneath, on a long, rough wooden shelf stood jam jars of flowers, one by each photograph. Not one jar contained the same kinds of flowers as any other. I sat down with my back to the photographs.

"There are two mattresses behind the curtain in that corner." She had a husky, beautiful voice. "I think you ought to go to sleep now; you've had more than enough to drink, and tomorrow the others are coming. But be careful you don't lie on top of Parson and Priest." I tried to push the cats off the mattress nearest the corner, because I preferred to lie close to the wall, but one of them, Parson as I learned later, hissed and scratched my hand, and so I lay down on the other mattress. Fay pulled the curtain aside and threw something to me. "Here's the table cloth," she said. "Wrap it around yourself. It's always chilly and damp in this wretched house."

I didn't know what time it was when I woke up, because long, dark shrouds of rain had shut out the land. My head was heavy with a headache. I walked dizzily to the window and looked into the rain. Suddenly I heard a brief, dry sound—the snipping of garden scissors—and then I saw Fay. She was standing barefoot on the sharp, gritty stones, cutting blooms from the wild rosebush. Her short hair was now bluish black because of the rain. She was wearing a mauve plastic coat and short black clothes underneath. I saw that she was more beautiful than any woman I had ever seen before, even more beautiful than the Chinese girl whom, admittedly, I hadn't seen for more than a minute in Calais. Later, on the island, I saw men go crazy over Fay. They did the most ridiculous things to draw her attention or to sleep with her. And even when they succeeded in this, either because she happened to be in the mood for it or because, as usual, she had been drinking, they ended up with nothing more than the painful memory of sharp strong teeth and total indifference on her part. Each time she selected a bloom to cut, critically and thoughtfully, I saw a characteristic movement of her mouth. She would draw her upper lip against her upper teeth and stick her lower jaw forward a little. Children sometimes do this, too, when they are pulling an insect apart. Because I had often seen her make that movement, I knew that it gave her face a cruel, devilish appearance. The ordinary expression of nonchalant bitterness or sarcasm in her eyes became intensified, and her eyes grew smaller and harder—and I think also blacker and more unapproachable than ever.

"Hello!" I called. She looked up and laughed. Fay rarely laughed, and the delicacy then revealed by her face was bewildering, for usually her face looked coarse owing to a melancholy that even the sarcasm in her eyes could not hide. "Wait a minute," I called, and ran downstairs. At the foot of the stairs I pulled off my outer clothes and socks and threw them onto a dry place that must have once been a verandah. "Can I help you?" I asked. The rain poured down my face, and my hair stuck in strands to my forehead.

Fay did not reply but pointed to a rhododendron bush and raised three fingers. She herself bent down over a cluster of sweet william and paid no further attention to me. Carefully, so as not to trip over a stone or slip on the mossy rock and wood, I clambered to the rhododendron bush and pulled off three flowers. The last, tough bit of stem I had to bite with my teeth. I spat out the bitter juice, but the taste stayed in my mouth.

I raised the heavy flowers to show them to Fay, who nodded approvingly. She cupped her hands around her mouth like a trumpet and called out, "Lilacs—four!" I looked about but saw no lilacs anywhere. "I can't see any lilacs," I called, but because it was raining so hard she couldn't hear what I said. I called again, "No lilacs." She replied, "Climb over the wall and cross the bridge." I pulled myself up on the ivy but was afraid that the winding branches and the moss would come away from the wall. Kicking and floundering, I groped for a foothold, but I could find nothing. The ivy stems cut sharply into my hands, and just when I was about to let myself fall, I felt two strong warm hands on my calves, pushing me up. I was soon at the top, and balancing on the crumbly stone, I turned and saw Fay holding out a hand to be hauled up. She didn't need more than one quick little pull. She planted her feet, their red nails glistening strangely against the green, in the ivy and climbed up like a cat.

On the other side was a dead stream that, with a few capricious fan-shaped curves, came to a green and brackish end in a pond full of slime and evil-looking water plants that rose warningly above the velvet surface. We let ourselves slide down the wall in order to reach the bridge, which consisted of two rough tree trunks linking the banks and crossed by a number of short logs laid in grooves.

Fay went ahead, jumping nimbly from log to log. Lumps of dirt and bark started to fall down, forming a small, rumbling avalanche that broke the dead water in front of us. I followed her but halted when I saw one of the logs wobble. I stuck my nails into the palms of my hands and hoped I would find the courage to go on before she reached the bank and looked around. I planted a stick I had found by the wall as firmly as possible against a knot in the right-hand trunk, and jumped. The log tipped, but before I could slip off, I jumped to the next. Panting, I reached the bank almost at the same time as Fay and felt the thumping of my blood in my temples and throat. She had already moved on to a kind of peninsula formed by the last baroque twist of the river, and when I arrived, she was inspecting the lilacs.

She handed me the scissors, and after examining the bush closely from all sides, she pointed to the chosen stems, one by one, and to the exact place on each stem where I was to snip. With an ape-like, deft movement of her left hand she caught the falling blooms. After I had cut four, she bent her head deeper into the bush; the beautiful line of her neck was fully extended from beneath the roughly cropped hair. Near the front of her neck, on the right-hand side, was an oblong scar left from an operation. She never concealed it, though she could have easily done so, and this, too, added to my sense of something wild and cruel about her. Whenever I saw her angry or in any other way agitated, I expected that scar to start bleeding.

As she stood there, I put my arm around her shoulders in a quick, timid gesture. "Come," I said. It was as if she were briefly startled, for she turned and held her hand around my neck, her nails pressing gently into my skin. She looked at me, and far from being cruel, her mouth and therefore her face now had something weak about it. The bitterness that was also there had lost all its power. When she spoke, the scar on her neck trembled slightly.

"You'd better go back," she said. "You'd better leave before the others arrive. This is a game with only losers. Of course"—her eyes withdrew further and further into a sorrow, or a weakness, that I could not follow—"of course, it's up to you."

"I don't know any games with winners," I said.

Her nails pressed deeper. "As long as you know," she said. The weakeness vanished and she started to laugh, but too loudly. Her body shook and she bent her head far back, like a bacchante on a Greek vase.

It was almost madness that glittered in her eyes. She flung the flowers on the grass and grabbed both sides of my head and bit me. She bit me on the mouth and the neck and wrenched my teeth open with hers. I screamed with pain, and suddenly she let me go and slowly walked backward, step by step. There was now some blood on her mouth, and she held her head to one side like a surprised dog. She made small, jerky movements with her hands and began to laugh again, but more softly now, almost demurely, and with her real voice, a contralto voice.

I picked up the lilacs and arranged them carefully according to length, but when I saw her walking back to the bridge and preparing to jump over the logs like a wildcat or God knows what, I yelled, "Go on, fall, fall!" She paused on the shaky log whose smoother side now faced upward because it had rolled over, and she stepped sideways, to the left-hand trunk, and with her legs wide apart and her back to the stream she pulled the log into the water. When, with much difficulty, I had reached the other bank with the lilacs, I climbed the wall and let myself slide down the other side along the ivy. Back at the house I could tell she was upstairs, because Parson and Priest were screaming at her.

I did not want to go upstairs yet, and went to the dry place on the verandah to put my clothes on. If I hadn't had cause to laugh before, I did now, for in a corner I found a stack of ridiculous drawings in wild colors by Jawson Wood—slightly mildewed and in antique, crested frames.

It was still raining. I combed the water out of my hair and thought what a long journey it had been from Digne to Luxembourg via Paris and Calais. There are big cities on that route, dirty cities that you are afraid of and that you ought to draw only with a gray pencil. When you arrive or leave early in the morning with the sun, a gray light spreads and the first people outdoors head for the trams and buses. They greet one another with a silent handshake or across the street with some call or other, and I walk in their midst.

On my way to Paris, one night I slept on a seat in a park in Grenoble. "If you go to the Routiers," said the man who dropped me there, "you're bound to find a truck going to Paris or Lyon." I didn't find one, for no one stopped to give me a lift. So I sat at a table close to the bar until two o'clock in the morning, drinking Beaujolais while a succession of drivers came in for a quick Pernod or cognac. They brought with them a sickening smell of oil and sweat. Outside the braking and starting of their heaving heavy vehicles resounded.

From time to time I went outside for a breath of air. The nocturnal game at a Routiers is fascinating, the trucks approaching from a distance with two huge headlights and, above the cabin, a third, vicious eye. When the long orange indicator swings out, you know that at the rear the red lights are also flashing, for this game has its rules and a mistake can be fatal. The engine roars once more and then falls silent. The cabin door ruptures the stillness of the night, and a man with a gray, unshaven face gives you a tired, impatient look as you ask for a lift to Paris.

They are not allowed to give lifts—the boss, you understand . . . an accident, the responsibility?—and they enter the café, shake hands, and drink and chat for a while. They hear the latest news about their fellow drivers from the girl behind the counter, and a moment later they are gone again, fighting on their own against the night, against sleep, against roads that are often too narrow for their colossal trucks.

I reached Paris in the end, but not until the next day, for after leaving the Routiers and sleeping on that park bench, I woke up stiff and cold and started walking out of Grenoble until a truck caught up with me. Instead of making the ritual thumb gesture, I waved my arms. He stopped.

"Paris," I shouted, but he could not hear, over the running engine.

"Paris," I shouted again. "Est-ce-que vous allez à Paris?"

He called from above, "Paris. Hurry up then. Allez vite, there's another truck behind me."

It was getting on toward five o'clock in the morning, and I was happy because this time I would be going to Paris. On the way south I had gone via Rheims, leaving Paris to my right. I think I felt like a Roman on his first visit to Athens.

The city itself was warm but not friendly to a stranger like me. I took the metro from Les Halles, where the driver had dropped me, to the Porte d'Orléans, for I had to go to the youth hostel near the Boulevard Brune. The metro was busy, and in the close, hostile atmosphere of the underground I felt dirty and tired. The ride was long, and I was glad to be above ground again. The youth hostel was about a ten minutes' walk from the metro, and I was just in time to register, for the doors are closed from ten to five. I wandered around Paris the entire day, feeling lost among all those people who passed me laughing and talking, and I fled past the statue of Henri IV to the Pointe de la Cité. The two arms of the Seine rejoin at the tip of the island, and when barges pass, the drab water laps against the stones.

I know it isn't fair to write about Paris in this way, for I had these thoughts, not on the verandah of Fay's house, but later, when the exhilaration of the Roman in Athens had faded, and even later, in the days of my poverty in this city and of all the other poverty which therefore surrounded me. But those days had not yet come.

Paris, the first time, was magnificent. The sun shone and I lay on the island quay listening to the water and to the city breathe behind the tall trees on the opposite banks. Soon after, I met Vivien, and she was the link with Calais. Everything was well ordered and this is still a story.

She laughed too loudly—that was it. We were in the youth hostel, and she laughed too loudly. But when I sought the face that laughed so, I found only an ordinary face with many lines around the eyes, as with people who have had a sorrow. It is ridiculous, I thought, that someone is so cheerful with such a face, and I told her so that evening.

It was a pleasant evening. There were Australians and Ellen, Vivien's friend, and a boy from Utrecht. Somewhere in the bar somebody was singing to the sounds of an accordion, and at the zinc counter the landlord washed the glasses with a clatter. There was a lot of smoke and, outside, everything was waiting for a thunderstorm.

"What are you thinking about?" asked Vivien. And suddenly I noticed she was stroking my hand. I looked at her. She is old, I thought. The Australians and Ellen left, but Vivien did not want to go with them. The boy from Utrecht stayed, too, because he had a night key. Vivien and I did not. "Why don't you say anything?" she whispered. She bent her head slightly forward toward the boy from Utrecht: "Three's a crowd."

In the metro, on the way back to the Porte d'Orléans, she kept stroking my hand, apparently enjoying it. I wished she wouldn't, because I thought it was merely ridiculous. This is not honest, because it is not true; but it *is* true that I thought so later, when she wanted me to kiss her and hold her. I was sure I wouldn't be able to do it properly, or at least not well enough, because she was older and I knew she had slept with many men even though she had not said so. Never mind. The key was outside; Utrecht was inside. I kissed her and felt how warm she was. Suddenly I noticed that I wasn't kissing her but she me, and that she was holding and stroking me. She said, and I could actually feel her voice because she was so close to me, "You're so strange. Your eyes . . ." Then she said no more and panted and let me go.

We walked slowly back to the Boulevard Brune and drank coffee in a bar. Some young workers were playing table football, and I have every reason to remember what they looked like. Two of them wore overalls, the other three cheap clothes in garish colors. The clatter of the table football and their raucous, inarticulate shouts drowned the Patachou records.

Two of the youths came to our table. "Are you Americans?" one of them asked.

"No—she is Irish, Irlandaise," I said. "I am Dutch."

"No," he said. "Americans." He was a bit drunk and called the others. "These are Americans," he said. And to us, "Have a coffee on us."

This seemed like what we had read about the Parisian character in the little book the boy from Utrecht had loaned us, and we accepted. She pressed my leg between hers under the table and I understood that she wanted to leave. I wanted to leave, too, though I was afraid the others would say something about it to each other, or laugh.

"The French proletariat," said one of the young workers, "offers a drink to American capitalism." The others laughed. They were now standing in a circle around us, watching us drink our coffee.

"Not Americans," I said. "She comes from Ireland, Dublin, and I come from Holland. La Hollande, Pays-Bas, Amsterdam."

"No," said the leader, the one who was tipsy.

"Americans. New York. How do you do, Americans, capitalists."

We finished our coffee, thanked them, and shook hands. They saw us to the door, and I noticed that they were still watching us when, farther down the road, she kissed me. I pulled her along. And suddenly I noticed they were walking behind us. "They're following us," I said. She looked around. They were gaining on us, and when we began to walk faster they started running. "Let's run for it," I said to her. "If we run fast, we'll get there before them. It isn't far." But she didn't want to run, and a moment later they had caught up with us. We stopped, and no one said anything. It was strange and frightening, the way they were standing around us, grinning.

At last the leader, who had offered us the coffee, spoke. He grabbed hold of me. "There's something the matter," he said. "It isn't serious, but, well . . ." He was really drunk now. "It's very disagreeable," he sighed. The others stood silently in a circle around us.

"What do they want?" asked Vivien. She didn't understand French.

"I don't know." I asked the man who was holding me, "What do you want? Let go." He grabbed me by the neck and shook me.

"Don't you give me a big mouth, you dirty American!" he shouted. "It's because you've got a bird with you." He slackened his grip for a moment. I was afraid.

"Let's run," I said to Vivien. But she asked again, "What do they want?" and I shouted, "I don't know, I told you, didn't I?"

The leader grabbed hold of me again. "There's a bit of a problem," he said. "Something to do with the till at the café. It doesn't tally. It's a small matter."

I realized I was very tired. There were no longer any people in the street. "It's very disagreeable," he whined again. "Very disagreeable. A small matter. Would you mind coming back to the café?"

"Okay," I said. "We'll ask the patron." We all started walking slowly in the direction of the café, dumb and silent like cattle, until they stopped again. I wanted to go on, but the leader started shouting. "Pack it in, you goddam filthy . . . ," but he was unable to finish.

"I thought we were going back to the café," I said, but he grabbed me by the clothes again and pushed his big fist against my mouth while another held a hand over my nose, cutting off my air. "If you hadn't had a bird with you," he yelled again, and he swore. Suddenly they let go of me, and he started whimpering and sniveling. "It's so awful, I can't explain."

I started walking slowly backward until I saw the knife that one of the others carried in his hand. It's just like real, I thought, and the knife is rusty. "How much?" I asked.

"Six hundred," they said.

"Six hundred," I said to Vivien, for I had no money on me.

"Why?" she asked, but I did not reply. "Ask them what's wrong."

"They're drunk," I said. "Can't you see?"

She took out her purse. "An Irishman would have fought the lot of them," she said. "One, two, three, four." She counted the hundred-franc notes into the waiting, sweaty hand.

"There are only four here," he said, "and you've got a one-thousand there."

"Ask him if he can change it."

In reply to my question he waved the four notes Vivien had just given him. She gave him the thousand-franc note, and he gave her the four hundred.

"That was awful," he said, and shook hands with us. He was really crying now. "Very bad, very bad."

Neither of us said a word. I knew she thought I was a coward, and after a while I asked her, "I suppose you think me a coward now?"

"No, I'm sorry about that," she said. "You're not a fighter, and anyway, what could you have done against five of them?"

Yes, I thought, that is true, and I found an even better

excuse. "God knows what they might then have done to you, since they were drunk." But, I thought, an Irishman would have fought. And she thought so, too, of course, but she stood still and said, "Let's forget all about it. It hasn't happened."

We walked on. The streets were silent, but in the distance we could hear the city. And because I knew she was waiting for it and because she kept touching my hand, I took her in my arms, pressed her against the wall, and stroked her; but I didn't stop thinking. I registered her face in minute detail—the soft down on her cheeks, the groping pink mouth. She began to move under my hands, swaying like yachts sometimes do when they catch the wind in a certain way. I heard her speak, but I couldn't hear everything she said.

"What's the matter?" I asked. "What are you saying?" I slowly let go of her.

She turned her head away from me and held her mouth open. She stood like that for a time. Then she asked, "How old are you?"

"Eighteen," I said.

"Who taught you?"

I didn't think I had done anything special. I had simply done it as I thought you were supposed to, or as I thought others did it, or whatever. "I've never slept with a woman," I said.

She took me by the shoulders and held me at a short distance. "Then don't, ever."

"You must have slept with lots of men," I said.

She nodded pensively, as if she were counting. "But I never will again." And suddenly she started to cry.

To tell the truth, I became furious. Not a very chivalrous reaction, but that was how it was. "Don't cry," I said. "Don't." I wondered, why do people always cry when they are with me, and for the first time I thought of my uncle Alexander again and of that first evening in Loosdrecht when he said he wasn't crying.

"I'm not crying," she said, "but how did you know I was sad?"

"Your eyes." I ran my fingertip around them as if I were drawing an eyeglass frame. "You have lines here." I remained bent over her while she leaned against the wall and cried.

At last she came out with it. "He was so beautiful," she said, singing out the final word and giving it an ecstatic sound.

"Who?" I asked.

"My baby."

So you're a mother, I thought. "I think I'd like to go to bed now," I said, but she wanted to tell me about the man who had left her in the lurch.

"He was so big and handsome and he did everything so well. I could easily have forced him to marry me—easily. He even offered it himself, though he didn't really want to. I didn't accept his offer because I loved him. What happened after that was nothing, painless by comparison." She lifted her head slightly and looked at me sharply. "You have strange eyes," she said again, "seductive eyes. I think they must be green in the daylight: they're cat's eyes."

They are all colors, I thought, and she put her hands under my clothes and said I should do the same to her. I felt how soft she was, and because I did not keep my hands still, she started to move again and to pant a little. I thought, if I don't want to hear you pant, I'll have to pant myself, and if I don't want to feel you move under me—by then we were lying on her raincoat in the grass—I shall have to move myself. I tried to do it the way you sometimes see it in the movies, and I also started snorting a bit and moving the way she did. I felt it was so ridiculous, and I kept thinking how old she was and how ordinary, and a mother; but I don't think she noticed it. At last I lay still, and she said, "How thin you are."

"The child," I asked, where is it?"

"I had to give it away," she whispered, and now she really was very sad. "I had to give him away, and now I will never be allowed to see him again. I had to promise I would never try to. He has been adopted now. He was the most beautiful baby you ever saw."

"Yes," I said.

"He was big and strong. He'll have a different name now, and he will never know that the other woman is not his mother, nor who I am. I had to give him away because I am a nurse in a big convalescent home, east of London. I live in, and I couldn't keep him when I went back there after he was born."

"Yes," I said, and stood up. I was cold and stiff and aching.

"Kiss me," she said, and I kissed her again, as hard as I could, because I had noticed that that was how she liked it best. Then I quickly ran indoors because I was tired and wanted to go to bed. She had a tent outside, together with Ellen.

The next day I saw something strange, something I had never seen before. I had agreed to meet Vivien at one o'clock in the afternoon by the big pond in the Luxembourg Gardens, on the side of the rue des Médicis. I was already there at eleven because I liked it there. I sat near the grass and watched the passersby. My hand-embroidered black and red Rumanian cap soon became the cause of a small adventure. Much later, when I was poor in this city, the same cap would indirectly help me to a dirty, badly paid, but much-needed job. I noticed that someone was staring at me, and that he, a young man, changed seats when I pretended not to look. After a while he got up again and passed behind my back. I waited for him to speak to me. His voice was soft, and even I could tell that he spoke with a foreign accent.

"Are you from Yugoslavia?" he asked.

"No," I replied, and I was sorry, for I could tell from his voice that he would have liked me to come from Yugoslavia. "No, I am Dutch, and this cap comes from Rumania." The fellow was a political immigrant. He told me about his country, and he gave me a ticket for a meal in one of the Foyers Israélites. I went there to eat with Vivien, for he himself had already eaten.

Vivien didn't seem quite so old that day, because she didn't want to; she looked as if she was determined to have fun and laugh a lot. The Foyer was crowded and noisy, but we liked that in those days, and we watched the Jewish boys, some of whom wore black yarmulkes like my uncle Alexander, and listened to all the languages that were spoken there. Afterward I would have liked to go to the Ile, but Vivien wanted to go back to the youth hostel.

"Why?" I asked. "It's closed until five."

"My tent isn't."

And as I went there with her, I saw her face begin to change. It was warm inside the tent, and she was lying close against me. She was silent, and I wasn't really looking at her. But later I lay on top of her and saw that her face had changed. It was young, and the sunlight that shone on the orange tent cloth gave it a bewildering orange glow. I definitely did not love her, because I thought I would love the Chinese girl if I ever found her. But the enchantment was there, and I gently passed my finger all over that strange face I had never seen before. The face shone, and it was as if I were not touching it at all, or even could touch it.

"Hey," I said softly as if I thought that maybe she had become as distant as her face. But she was still there, and I said, "Hey, your face has changed."

She laughed gravely. "How?" she asked.

"I don't know." I was trying to work it out. "It's younger. And I think it's beautiful."

She went on laughing, a little enigmatically, and therefore she was no longer ordinary. She looked happy. She lifted her arms, and although she laughed, she really meant something different when she said, "You hadn't seen this before, had you?"

"What?" I hadn't seen anything.

"I shouldn't really tell you this," she said, "because I am sorry about it—it was cowardly." By then I had noticed the two strange stripes on the insides of her elbows.

"How?" I asked.

She turned her head so I could no longer look at her. "With a razor," she said. "But it was when I was in the hospital; I hadn't found the vein properly, and they found me so quickly I didn't get the chance to bleed to death."

"I see," I said, and although the face was still far away, I carefully went over it with my mouth. She had wanted me to sleep with her, I knew, though she obviously thought I was a coward after that evening when I didn't fight, and though I wasn't really as handsome and as big as other men and probably couldn't lie on her as well. But however that may have been, we couldn't, because Ellen came in and the next day they were leaving.

That evening we decided to have a race to see who would be in Calais first, hitchhiking. We—that was Geneviève, an American girl; the two Australians; Ellen; Vivien; and I. I didn't really want to go to Calais at all, since I had no money to go to England anyway, but I knew that after Vivien had gone, there would be no one left here that I knew. This has always remained the same in all my travels. I am always a loser because I attach myself too much to things or to people; and so traveling is no longer traveling but taking leave. I have spent all my time taking leave and remembering, and collecting addresses in my diaries, like small tombstones.

The next day I got up at six o'clock. Paris was morose and unpleasantly chilly. I didn't know whether I was the first to leave, but I was determined to be in Calais that evening, for I wanted to prove to myself that I belonged to the others and that I was taking part in the race. All through that day I imagined that they would be there that evening, too. I did not doubt for a moment that the girls would arrive before me.

I took the metro to the Porte de la Chapelle and from there a bus in the direction of Saint Denis. It had begun to rain gently, and there were no trees, so I got wet and dirty. Besides, I didn't want to start hitching right away, for as long as there are still houses along the road, I always have a feeling that people are watching me from behind their curtains, which is usually true. I didn't have much luck that day—nothing but short lifts. There was not much traffic, and I sometimes had to walk for long distances with my heavy pack, among wheat fields and pastures. It was impossible to lie down or even sit, because everything was wet from the drizzle. It was very quiet, walking there, all on my own.

My first lift had taken me to Chars, which is really off the route that runs via Beauvais, and so I had little choice but to go to Gournay and then from there to Abbeville. A big truck picked me up.

"Everything is corrupt!" the driver shouted to me. "Parliament, the ministers, everybody."

"Yes," I replied, and his cargo and the loosened, trembling metal of the cabin applauded emphatically on the bad stretch of road. We smoked our gitanes, and I tried very hard to follow him and to say yes or no at the right moments, for which he seemed to wait before continuing his tirade.

"And the worst of it is that these ministers, even if they've been in the saddle for no more than a week . . . "

Would Vivien be in Amiens yet, I wondered, or would she be taking the same route as I?

". . . draw a fat pension for the rest of their lives."

"Yes," I said, and I decided to ask him if he had seen two girls, one of them with a little Irish flag. He swore because the windshield wipers weren't working, for the rain was getting heavier now and lashed viciously against the windshield, forcing him to slow down.

"And then this war!" he called. "Costing us a billion francs every day. Aha-ha-ha, c'est trop intelligent, l'homme, même plus que les bêtes. Merde." He paused until we came to a pothole in the road that would cause his words to receive the fullest acclaim from both truck and cargo, and with outstretched arm, he gazed at a road almost invisible through the rain and called out prophetically, "France is finished. Europe is finished."

At least I got to Calais. From drab, desolate Boulogne in a greasy, smelly oil tanker, to even drabber Calais—along a road over which heavy banks of mist came drifting in from the sea. It was as if the truck cabin could scarcely bear the pressure of the hopelessness and squalor outside. It was eight o'clock when my driver dropped me in the center. "Au revoir."

"Yes, au revoir." The rain was clattering down, and the streets were dirty and full of puddles. A boy in a short leather coat and blue jeans watched me as, avoiding the puddles as much as possible, I went up to him. He had a hard, spiteful face and a short mangy beard.

"Could you tell me where the youth hostel is?" I asked, wiping the water from my eyes. He looked at me for a while without answering. Then he spat forcefully into a puddle and said, "It's three kilometers up the road you've just come from. I'm going there, too. You can follow me." I asked him if he had seen two girls, one Irish and one English, but he spat again, said "No," and started walking.

My clothes clung to my body, and as I had not eaten anything that day, I felt sick. He walked ahead of me in the rain, which battered against my face until my skin was numb and as cold as marble. Every so often he spat with a raw scraping sound of his throat, and he did not speak. I hated Calais. The road we walked on was covered in sand and coal grit, the soil was soaked and spongy, and the houses stood apathetically and wretchedly in the falling rain. From behind dingy curtains, dirty children with pale adult faces watched us without any discernible emotion other than boredom. Every now and then there were gaps between the houses, wastelands littered with offal and rusty iron, and a filthy dog barking angrily at us, defending in advance the garbage he might be able to scratch from somewhere.

The youth hostel was on a side street, off the road to Boulogne. It was a low wooden building, and there was no one there. I had won the bet, and I was sad because I would now spend the evening alone with the Algerian, for that was what he was. I thought I would probably eat at the same table as he and that he would say nothing, only spit. Toward ten o'clock one of the Australians arrived, a big, red-faced fellow with a Henry the Eighth beard. Although I had hardly noticed him in Paris, I now felt more at home. He had heard nothing of Ellen and Vivien, nor of the others. "Maybe," he said, "they caught the six o'clock boat to Dover." Then they are already in England, I thought, and I shall not see them again.

Later in the evening more hitchhikers entered. They brought rain with them in their clothes, and the memory of a miserable day; but Vivien was not with them, and no one had seen her. I was cold that night because I didn't have enough blankets, and I was glad when day came; but it brought only more rain, and my clothes were still wet. Outside it was gloomier than ever. That night while we were asleep, the other Australian had arrived. He hadn't seen Vivien, and it now seemed certain that she would not come. The Australian asked me to come with them to drink up their last French francs, and I did. It was a small eating house near Rodin's *Burghers of Calais.* We ate nothing but french fries, and afterward we each drank a bottle of cheap Algerian wine.

The last toast was to Vivien because she was in England. But she wasn't in England, for when we arrived arm in arm at the passport control at the harbor, she was queuing up near customs. She had only got as far as Boulogne the night before. "Vivien!" I called, "Vivien!" But she said I was drunk, and I started to cry because I was sure it wasn't true. I wanted to kiss her, but she gently pushed me away and said I had better wave goodbye from the beach. "All right," I said. "I'll wave goodbye to you from the beaches of France."

But I could not find any beaches of France because there were houses everywhere, and by the port there was no beach. I asked someone where the beach was, the French beach, but they did not understand me and so I went on walking to where I thought the sea would be, behind the houses. At last I found it, and it was quiet, and rather sad in the rain. And England lay faintly in the distance, floating on the waves.

I woke up from the sound of a ship's siren, but it was not from the one o'clock ferry that Vivien was on; it was from a later one. Although it was early June, it was already dark because of the rain and the corpselike color of the sky. Three times the siren blew, sounding like an old, melancholy elephant. As I lay on the shore, I saw the boat sailing away. It wasn't Vivien's boat, I knew; but my hand, which had wanted to wave, briefly remained raised in the air in a foolish, frozen gesture. I got up slowly. My clothes were heavy with rainwater, and I had a splitting headache. "Vivien," I said, "Vivien." But I laughed aloud because I hadn't cared for her a bit. I roared with laughter and slapped my thighs with my hand so that the water splashed out of my pants, for I had been lying in the rain for six hours. And I laughed because I was sick and because she had an old face and had wanted me to kiss her.

Then I noticed that someone was watching me and I froze. The laughter vanished fearfully from the beach and there was no more sound, except that of the sea and a few screeching gulls. I turned and saw her for a fleeting moment. She was wearing tight black cords without cuffs and a dark-gray anorak above which the high black collar of a woolen jersey was visible. Her short black boyish hair was dull and tousled from the rain. Her hair was the color of crow's feathers, and her eyes were very big and brown in her narrow Chinese face.

I knew that this was the girl, even though she was like a small, earnest boy. She was so near me that I could almost touch her. Yes, I could see very clearly that she was opening her mouth as if to say something, but then she suddenly took a step backward because I had moved, and she started to run away. She climbed on a dune and looked down at me for a moment. I had not followed her because I could not run fast in my heavy, wet clothes. "Don't go," I called out, "don't go. Wait for me."

But she disappeared behind the dune, and I was alone again with the sand and the sea. Slowly I too began to walk back, following her footsteps until I came to a road.

2

That was the first road on which I followed her. But after that?

At first her footprints could still be seen in the wet sand of the dunes near Calais, and later there were people who had seen her in Luxembourg or in Paris or Pisa. But what does it matter, really? It is a story, and I once told this story to a friend but, mark you, in the third person—*and slowly he too began to walk back, following her footsteps*—and then it became a story about someone else and no longer about me, for I didn't want this to have happened to me.

Another, not I, when he finally arrived at the youth hostel, heard that she had arrived that night after everyone else—and that she had already left again. Where to? Nobody knew, for in the register she had put a question mark after that question. So it was another, not I, who wrote the names of the big European cities on a piece of paper and then blindly pointed his finger at the paper. It happened to point at Brussels, and he therefore left the next day, knowing that it was not another, but I, hitchhiking from Calais to Dunkirk.

And why? Why was I not sitting in an office, like others? Why did I stand by the roadside in the rain while they worked? A road. I now know what a road is, because I have seen and known many of them, bathed in red and pink by a first and last sun, tapering to an end at a horizon embraced by rain, crumbling and cracking and covered in choking dust that whirls around me, wayfarer, and creeps into my pores. Or, twisting and turning with a face harsher than the surrounding mountains, embedded in the secrets of forests, suddenly changing from day road to night road with the longing that goes with this—all are roads on which to walk when you have already walked for so long and grown tired. Tired.

And did I therefore become less lonely? Because people gave me lifts and talked to me? Surely I may ask myself this: did I therefore become less lonely because people took me with them and gave me food and drink?

Dic nobis Maria, quid vidisti in via, "What did you see on the road?" *Mors et vita duello conflixere mirando,* "Death and life in a wondrous struggle," for that is the image people present, a picture of life and death in a wondrous struggle—I who sought a Chinese girl everywhere and had lost her, and those who did not seek her but who gave me lifts while they sought something else, and then I again, wanting to sit down quietly to think about these things. But I had already seen far too much, and the road is restlessness, forever and ever, for it is clear that I have understood life badly and spent it worse. And yet, the outcome is the same:

"What are you doing?"

"I am looking for a girl."

"What kind of girl?"

"A girl with a Chinese face. I can't help it."

No one must get angry with me. I am only a child, and I have stood for too long in the evening (who said that?). I am looking for a girl. She must be somewhere here, or maybe in Rome, maybe in Stockholm or Greece—at any rate, near here.

"What are you doing?"

"I am looking for a girl, what kind of girl, a girl with a Chinese face. Yes, once, I've seen her once. That was on the beach at Calais."

"No, never before."

Yes, maybe once, but I am no longer sure, because it wasn't

real. Perhaps I only imagined it; an old man told me of it—Maventer. He took me to a village I do not know the name of, and his hands were as soft as molluscs, and his arms were white and fat and hairless.

It is raining but I go on. I cannot stop now. My unquiet heart of St. Augustine in the unquietness of the cities or of the journey. Yes, I am looking for something. A girl? Yes, a Chinese girl. Maybe I am looking for something different. This is a farmhouse. I have been standing here for six hours, but Belgians don't stop. I am a beggar, but beggars are out of fashion here. Why are you restless? All these welfare provisions—is this life not the real life, and is there not another world? Well, I can't see it myself, but if you say so. However, this is a farmhouse and perhaps I shall be allowed to stay the night here, but you may be sure that this is not the world. A paradise lives beside it. I have peeped into it.

I was allowed to stay the night, in the hayloft. Hand over my passport, hand over my matches, the dog yelping and whining on his chain and then looking at me mockingly and mistrustfully. But they did allow me to stay the night, for it had become evening again, and it was a long way to the next village. The hay was warm and itchy. I hid under it in a corner, for there are many noises in and around a farm that I do not know. Strange sounds that come toward you, concealed by the night and with the wind from the tall trees behind them, perhaps talking to that wind with long, groaning mouths. But I didn't want to listen to them, and I felt the hay with my hands, so that it would be easier to imagine that it had once been green and alive, that it had bowed under the rain, like me.

But it became deader and deader, until it could no longer even hold the memory of the sun. It is dead, I thought, and if I had not guessed that it was the dog outside, dragging his chain over the ground, I would have screamed in fear, because I was lying underneath dead bodies, under corpses that covered me like earth. I leaped up and knocked the hay off myself as if it were dangerous, but when I stood still, panting, I heard only how it fell rustlingly about my feet. I lay down again, wondering how I would get to Brussels and thinking that she would probably not be there anyway.

Toward the afternoon of the following day I was in Brussels. It wasn't raining that day. On the contrary, it was warm with a stifling oppressiveness, as if a storm were brewing. I had a good deal of difficulty in finding the youth hostel, and when I learned that she was not there, nor had been, I had to find the way out of the city again, because I did not know where to find her in such a big place. But where should I go? I chose Luxembourg, and why not—I had the same chances everywhere.

A big town on the route is a nightmare to the poor little hitchhiker. The kind of town you never stay in, such as Lille or Saint Etienne, can cost you hours—hours of asking the way, going wrong, going right, before you are safely on the other side, on the main road once again. A lift to Wavre, another to Namur, walking through names while the air becomes warmer and a town is no more than houses and heat, the weight of a rucksack and weariness.

And then another lift. Talking. But this man tells you something. His wife has left him. Why does he tell me this? Because he doesn't know me. He drives on and I stay behind. Why shouldn't he tell me? I am just a stranger and it gives him relief. Twenty kilometers before Marche he turns left. Dusk is falling and it is beautiful here. These trees are firs, and when I walk on, I come to a castle. It shimmers in its moat, and where the walls touch the water, the gauze shrubs of a small mist move as though trying with childish waves of the hand to blur the outlines and to suggest that the castle is a flower, floating on the bated breath of the water surface.

No cars pass me now, and I think the castle will walk around me and grab me from behind, sweetly, but it is bobbing gently, on which breeze? And it sails on the water of the moat, watching me through the big eyes of its windows.

A motor breaks the spell. It is a truck, and it stops without being asked.

"Where are you going?" shouts the driver.

"Luxembourg!"

"Come on! Get in!"

Later we no longer speak French but German. The man left Remich early in the morning with a heavy load of barrels of wine that had to be taken to Antwerp, and he is now returning with empty ones. He is on his way home, and very tired, so I light his cigarette for him and put it in his mouth, as you help a small child to eat his dinner. He asks me to talk to him, for he is afraid of falling asleep. And I do talk to him, but I have to shout; otherwise, he can't hear me above the noise of the barrels in the back and the heavy roar of the engine.

I shout until my throat is hoarse and raw, and he listens and answers, about the weather, the roads, the people. In Marche he stops and we have a beer. After Marche there is roadwork for a long distance, and I see how the sweat pours down his face and runs into his clothes as he forces the heavy truck along a single track of dirt and gravel, the headlights boring the darkness ahead, conquering meter after meter of the night. Then we stop again for a drink and so it goes on. He drives for a while, and when his eyes begin to droop, we stop for a drink in one of the little cafés along the road, where he chats with the people. They know him; he often passes. Twice every week the struggle with the last hundred kilometers. Driving, stopping, entering into a small world of light and drink, and if there are others, a game of billiards.

"Au revoir Madame, au revoir Monsieur"—and then driving again until his eyes, heavy and treacherous, threaten to close. The grip of his hands on the immense steering wheel slackens. In Steinfort we drank a glass of Remicher wine, but when he starts on his second game of billiards, I decide to phone the youth hostel.

"Who's speaking?" the voice is far away.

"Vanderley," I say.

"Who?"

"Has a girl with a Chinese face arrived?"

"Pardon?"

"A Chinese girl. *Chinese.*"

But there is no further answer. So she is not there; otherwise, the voice wouldn't have thought that I was drunk, or something like that.

As we drive on toward Luxembourg, it occurs to me that I don't really have to go there anymore. But he asks, "Where in Luxembourg do you want to be dropped?" and I say, "Grand-Duchess Charlotte Avenue," because there is bound to be one, and I have no idea where else I should go.

He even made a detour for my sake and dropped me on the corner of Grand-Duchess Charlotte Avenue. He drove off and I waited until I could no longer hear the noise of the truck, and the silence closed again over the houses. Then I slowly started walking back to the city center, because I thought there would be a signpost for Paris. And maybe that is where I would have gone if I had not met Fay.

I was already outside the town, where the woods begin and the night would not last much longer. Of course it was raining, because rain is closer to the night than anything else. She stopped in front of me in her small sport car and shone a flashlight into my face. She said, "Dans Arles, où sont les Alyscamps," and I didn't care that she knew, or how and why she knew. I took off my rucksack and put it on the backseat, and she turned the car and drove back through Luxembourg again, to this house ("That isn't a house," I said as we entered the drive, "and I don't even know your name." "Fay," she said. It was a ruin.), to this verandah where I am sitting now, after having picked flowers together with her. I look at the rain as at a friend. Why shouldn't I play with it?

"Yes," said the rain, "will you come out to play?" And we went out together, and the rain showed me how it opened the water in the moat and closed the flowers. It always walked quickly ahead of me, and tapped against the shrubs with its small hands. "Lift me on your shoulders," it said, "lift me on your shoulders," and I did, and that was why I was so wet when Fay called out that the others had arrived.

3

I don't know exactly why, but he reminded me of limestone. He was standing in front of the mirror when I came upstairs.

"What are you doing?" I asked.

"I'm pretending to be Narcissus," he said, and his voice was dry and without much sound, as if someone were rubbing two pieces of limestone against each other.

"I'm pretending to be Narcissus," he said. "It's fun. Narcissus dans les Alyscamps." He laughed like scraping limestone, sharp and dry. "How do you know about that?" I asked, and he laughed again and said, "A certain Maventer."

Fay and the other boy, who was tall and fat, were sitting by the table. "Hi-hi," the other boy said to me, "you must listen carefully to what he says. He has seen a lot and he knows a lot."

"Who are you?" I asked. "I don't know you."

"I am Sargon," he replied, "but I'm not coming until later."

The boy in front of the mirror raised his eyebrows and made his eyes grow big and round so that they lay like pale wilted flowers in the barren pallor of his face. "Oh, Narcissus," he said, "how ugly you are," and he held his hands in front of his face as if he did not want to see it any more, but he still looked through the slits of his eyes. "These hands are cold," he said, "and when it comes to it, dead. They don't belong to me." He turned, and the lugubrious orange glow of his eyes enclosed me like the light of an old-fashioned reading lamp.

"Of all limbs, the hand has the most independent life," he whispered. "Do you know that poem by Wildgans . . . 'ich weisz von deinem Korper nur die Hand' . . . look, it's alive." And we looked at the hand he had laid on the table, and it lay there, white and dead. He spoke to me again. "I, or rather my special case, can be categorized in many ways." He went to the mirror and wrote with his finger on the glass as if it were a school blackboard, but nothing appeared on it.

"Do you understand that?" he asked.

"No," I said.

"Have you any soap?" he asked Fay, and she gave him some. He wrote with it on the mirror, *morbus sacer*.

"Holy sickness?" I asked.

He nodded approvingly at me and pursed his mouth. "A dangerous holiness," he said. "Saints are dangerous to the people around them, and in homage to holiness, the Middle Ages called a danger holy: *morbus sacer, epilèpseia*." He wrote it on the mirror—*hè epilèpseia*—and under it the same word three times, *aura, aura, aura*. By each of these words he drew something: an eye, an ear, a nose. "Choose one," he said. But I did not move, because I didn't understand anything of it. "Don't just stand there," he yelled. "You have to choose one." I saw that he wasn't really angry and that he was merely on the verge of tears, and therefore I pointed my finger at the *aura* above the eye. "How did you know?" he asked, and walked out of the room.

The boy called Sargon followed him and shouted, "Heinz, come back, come back, Heinz. It's only a coincidence."

Fay got up and came toward me. She briefly put her arm around me. "They're crazy," she said, and let some water run into a pail, to wash the mirror. "I've heard it twice now, so I can tell it to you. That," and she pointed at *hè epilèpseia*, "is what he has, and that is all. The beginning of a seizure is called the aura, he says. It lasts only a very short time, a second or so. Some people hear a rustling or a whistling." She pointed to the ear. "And others see flames or stars, which is the case with him. That is all."

"That is not all," said Heinz, who had reappeared. "That isn't all by any means; it's only the beginning. I've read up on it to find out exactly what happens afterward."

"Shut up," said Fay, but he went on.

And then I have a spasm, a tonic spasm—a nice word, that." He laughed and repeated "Tonic." Fay slapped him in the face, but he roared with laughter and swayed back and forth in his chair and shouted, "and then the clonic one and then I shake. You don't have to hit me again," he said to Fay. "It's finished. At least, that's what it says in the book. Deep, deep sleep."

Fay shrugged her shoulders and continued cleaning the mirror. "Clean it properly," he said, "clean it properly. Otherwise, I can't see Narcissus any longer, and Narcissus and I have been through so much together." He ran his hands up and down his arms, rubbing them as if he wanted to make them warm; but his flesh was cold and white. "Long ago," he said to me, "I wanted to enter a monastery—I'll tell you from that corner over there." He went to the corner farthest from us. "I want to sit well away from you, because it happened a long time ago, when I didn't belong to you people yet." He passed his hands across his mouth as if to cast a spell on it.

"That other world," he said, "was much happier. I was a young child in it, and we were Catholics. Even after my father had been transferred from Bavaria to Hamburg, we always said the rosary before going to bed in the evenings and the Angel of the Lord at mealtimes. There were always flowers by the statue of Our Lady, and by the Most Sacred Heart there was always a little red light burning. The statue of the Sacred Heart was splendid in its cheapness. My mother had bought it at the flea market for three marks after the old one had broken, and the bits where the paint had flaked off, my father touched up with colored chalk. In brief, we were, as they say, a Happy Family. Later I went to school with the Carmelites.

Well"—and he shifted his chair slightly, startling us—"maybe we all have a time we call the happiest of our lives. It probably wasn't, and we were probably just as unhappy then as in the times we call unhappy, but it is a fact that we prefer to have happiness behind us rather than before us; it makes everything so much simpler. So my happiness lies in a provincial village. It is a small village and people were friendly. Outside the village there is a monastery, and opposite the monastery, on the other side of the street, the school. Go and look, and you'll find them, my memories.

"At a quarter to six in the morning the bells of the monastery rang with a sober, single sound. I would wake up and see that the others were still asleep. They were far away and sometimes happy, because some of them laughed and said things in their sleep. At five minutes to six the alarm went off in the duty master's cell, which was built in such a way that whoever was on duty could survey the two dormitories. At a quarter past six he would enter the dormitory with his bell. I can still hear that bell, though it is a long time ago. Ta-ding, ta-ding, ta-dingdingding. And he'd be standing by his door, ringing and saying, "Benedicamus domino," and we would say, "Deo gratias." Then he would walk past the beds and pull the blankets off anyone still asleep or pretending to be.

"All those sounds! For after the bell ringing and the getting up, the monk would walk past the washstands and shut the upper windows by pulling long cords. When he had finished with us, he would go to the dormitory of the little ones, where we used to be, before coming to Syntaxis or Rhetorica, and you could hear the bell again in the distance and the windows slamming shut, clap-clapclap. But by that time I was already at the washstands, for I had made a bargain with myself. There were those who were always first at the washstands and who then went back to bed to read for a while, but I washed and dressed in five minutes and checked whether the duty master was watching. Usually he was walking up and down the dormitory aisle, reading his breviary. When his back was to me, I quickly slipped out of the door. Our dormitory was in the attic, so I had to go down many stairs to get to the garden. I was always careful that no one discovered me, for it was forbidden to go into the gardens before mass. They weren't gardens, really; they were two fields. The Big Field and the Little Field."

He paused awhile and rose. He went to the boarded-up window and scratched on it with his nail, a ghastly sound. "The Big Field," he whispered, "what is it to you? Why do you bother to listen? Do you care whether I first crept past the wall of the bike shed in the playground because I had to make sure some priest wasn't there reading his breviary?" He went back to his chair.

"I once looked at a theosophical journal and I didn't understand it. Every profession, every religion, every group has its own jargon, and so did we, but it was a jargon of ordinary words. The Tree. After the Big Field you turned left, down the path that runs around the Little Field, and then the third tree along was The Tree." He turned to us again. "Start digging and you'll find them. Rusty cigarette cans with written masses inside them. The spoken part of the masses in church consists of prayers that are the same every day, as well as prayers that vary according to the day, that belong to a particular feast day or to a particular purpose.

I was a member of the mass committee, whose task it was to make up Latin prayers in the form of real prayers but for the more profane purposes of the other students. I made up large numbers of such prayers, to kindle the love of X, seen in the street on such and such a date or for Y, not to have a test paper. *Oremus, amorem magnam quaesumus Apollone, mente puellae infunde* . . . etcetera. It had been mutually agreed that these prayers would be addressed only to the ancient Greek gods, because some of the boys were afraid they might be blasphemous otherwise. The prayer, which was paid for with candy or sausage, had to be worn on the chest like an amulet, and when the favor had been granted, it was solemnly buried in a cigarette can under The Tree and witnessed only by the very few initiated.

"So there was a time when I was happy—happy standing around a tree with a few other boys, burying a can with a piece of paper inside it. Happy because we drank water from a bottle after first pouring a little on the ground, the obligatory libation to the gods." He laughed. "If you weren't here now, if you were now to leave, I could say all this in a small voice, as if it were not me talking, but someone else talking to me. Someone who would say to me, 'Do you remember how wet everything was in the morning, in that garden? The sun was born anew each time, in the drops in the grass and in the flowers, so that it looked as though small new suns were starting to flower on the green until in the end the gardens held their breath in rapture. And when it rained, you would stand under a tree, because you mustn't be seen turning up in chapel in drenched clothes. So you'd be standing under that tree looking at the rain, and you'd be singing because it was raining, because you liked the rain, didn't you?'"

He broke off again and waited until he was able to speak in his normal voice once more, for he seemed to be afraid of being happy with a memory. But the story repeatedly got the better of him, and then his voice rose from its ashen dryness, becoming young and vibrant as if touched with emotion, and his eyes glistened—until he remembered us again and returned to himself.

"So now you know," he said. "Now you know: the Big Field and the Little Field, the masses, The Tree. I could stay in the garden for only ten minutes, until the bell rang for mass. That was my signal to go quickly back to the dormitory and take my place in the rows of silent boys, each row with its own supervisor. We came out of our respective dormitories on our way to the chapel, which, like the statues at home, was lovely in its ugliness. The windows and Stations of the Cross were banal and the vestments were cheap, except on feast days such as Corpus Christi or Ascension Day. Then the bare, damp walls behind the altar were suddenly alive with palm branches and flowers, and the priests, in their heavy brocade robes, bowed, prayed, and sang in clouds of incense shot through with multicolored beams of sunlight as if in a mysterious game—for to me it was no more than that—enlivened by sometimes wistful, sometimes exuberant Gregorian chants."

We wondered how he would conclude this memory, and he said, "Perhaps I didn't think it was beautiful at all, at the time. Perhaps I thought the celebrant couldn't sing, or that the flowers were wilting, or that it was stuffy because of the cheap incense. Maybe I didn't even like being at school, where I had to get up at six and walk in a long crocodile to the chapel and kneel for an hour with my bare knees on a hard wooden bench, and then walk back in the same long crocodile, still in silence, to the study room. In winter it was cold in there, when we entered in the morning." He rubbed his hands as though he felt cold, and then he sat still with his hands between his back and the back of the chair.

"Now I know why I must have been happy there, especially in the winter when the seats were cold in the morning and we wore all the clothes we had so as to stay warm in that chilly building. We—that was why I was happy. Because I belonged. Now I no longer belong; I no longer belong anywhere. Not to other people, who feel cold—cold in different ways—all in their own compartments."

He went to the mirror and gave it a little push, and it started swaying back and forth. "Oh Narcissus," he said, "just press a button. There are so many—one button for the Big Walk on the Principal's Day or on the great feast days of the church. In the lower grades we used to play at robbers on the Big Walk in the woods. In the higher grades we were busy putting the world to rights. Another button: compulsory recreation on the Big Field on summer evenings. We worked in our little gardens or played badminton. Sometimes we sat reading on the benches under the poplars or walked across the width of the path, six paces forward, six back. I haven't seen anyone walking backward since then. After that, the war came.

"Narcissus wasn't allowed to join the army. Not even this army wanted Narcissus. 'No, Narcissus,' they said. 'You are sick. The State doesn't mind taking riffraff, but you are sick. We are scared of you. *Morbus sacer.* Amen.' Scared," he said to the mirror, which was still swaying. "Scared. Ay-ay. Too much has been said about the war. Even now there are people who think they have to write books about it. About bombings. I've been through those. About fires. I've seen them. About dead fathers and mothers—not merely dead, no, but really *destroyed,* smashed up. Mine were, too. About lawless youth, neglected children. I was one of them, later. About gangs among the rubble. That was where I belonged. But what do you expect? To me it was important to take a leap back and to let other memories prevail. But what can you do? I took a huge step, right across the whole burned out, devastated city of Hamburg, until once again I walked down corridors whenever a bell was rung, and sang in a choir when another bell was rung.

"Of course, I can be explained, more or less anyway. *Sensus clericus,* for instance, a fairly good approximation. So I went, paying for my journey with stolen money. Can you imagine it?" He put the mirror on his lap and looked into it. "Now I laugh," he said. "Now I laugh." He ran his fingers over his face. "Now they've gone," he laughed. "These wrinkles have gone. I am not beautiful yet, but I gleam. My eyes are still ugly, but they sparkle now, because I am on my way to my youth. I am already far away from the town where the train from Hamburg took me. It is almost evening. It is Christmas Eve, and I gleam in the windows. Outside, there is loneliness, and behind the loneliness there is a village where I have to get out. Beyond the village there is more loneliness. It has been snowing, and the silence whispers under my feet.

"No one can deny it—there had to be snow, and it had to crunch softly under my shoes. The moon had to be there; it had been hung in the sky for my sake, because I was going back to my youth. Even the bells of the Trappist monastery were part of it, and they tolled not for the inmates but for me. The monastery was still a long way off, safe and invisible in the embrace of the night that had its back to me. And somewhere inside it a monk stood pulling a bellrope, not knowing he was doing it for me. It is not my fault that I didn't go to the monastery with the same motive that led other men to enter. The others loved God, I am sure of that, because I have seen it; but honestly, honestly, I did not know that Man. Those others were there to pray that the world might turn to God, and to atone for the sins of mankind, but I thought that it would be of no use anyway, that the world would quietly carry on being sinful and never turning to God. From the monks' point of view, if they had known it, I would have been an impostor, a blasphemer. From the world's point of view I was a fool, neither more nor less.

"It was a hard life, certainly, getting up at two o'clock in the morning to meditate and to sing matins and lauds; but I was happy because I was part of a long white, silent procession, fasting, singing, working on the land, and I belonged. I also had a shaven head and a white habit with sleeves down to the ground. When I didn't have to look in my breviary because it was a well-known psalm that was sung every day, I could, standing in my tall choir stall, see myself in the opposite stall, responding each time I had sung my line. All day I was surrounded by myself. I saw myself during the hours, in the corridors, in the refectory. I was like an actor playing an everlasting part that no one could take away from me.

"I had been there for three months when I had my first seizure, still six years from ordination. But there was to be no ordination. 'Sorry, Narcissus,' they said, 'you are sick. It isn't possible to ordain priests that are sick. God must have intended you for the world after all. Goodbye, Narcissus, goodbye.'" He threw a matchbox at the ceiling and said, "You there, up there, if you are there, couldn't you have let me in because of my perseverance? I went to two more monasteries after that, small ones, very remote, until the game was up. Because the situation had stabilized after the war, I could no longer profit from the confusion in their organization. I was known. There was a dossier about me. It was the end."

He came toward me, and more than ever I was reminded of limestone and of everything that is dry and barren. "Now you know who I am," he said, "but not why I am here, not what my connection is with this girl. Maybe you'll know why I am hitching all around Europe if you have understood my story. You may assume that I probably passed through Arles as well, où sont les Alyscamps.

"And that is another story," he said in a different voice, and he gestured toward the boy who called himself Sargon.

"No," I said, "I don't want to hear. I don't want to hear any more." I went to the mattress on which I had slept the night before.

"You must listen." Sargon's voice came from behind the curtain. "You don't have to look at me, but you must listen."

"No," I called out, but he began anyway.

"Maybe it is a disappointment to you that my real name is not Sargon but John. I have called myself Sargon after the famous Assyrian king Sargon II, who conquered Samaria in 722 BC. Not *because* he conquered Samaria. That is, in the first place, of very relative importance after several hundred years, and secondly, it isn't so very different from Tiglath Pilesar I conquering the surrounding country in about 1200 BC, and Tiglath Pilesar III capturing Babylon, and Sargon taking Syria, and Assur even taking Egypt, and Psammichetus liberating Egypt again, and the Chaldeans reconquering Babylon, and the Mede Cyaxares destroying Assur in 164 and, two years later, Nineveh, so utterly that our dear Xenophon never even heard of those cities. No, it wasn't for that reason. I did it simply because I liked the name. Are you listening?" he asked. "Are you listening?"

"Yes," I said. "I'm listening."

"It's all because of the announcer, the announcer's voice. That is what it all started with, my story, though I don't remember exactly when I discovered that that was what I lived for. Do you think that is strange," he asked from the other side of the curtain, which swayed because he had brushed against it, "that someone lives for the voice of an announcer? Perhaps it was strange. Perhaps I even thought so myself, the first time someone asked me why I switched on the eight o'clock news when I had already heard it at six o'clock and at seven. 'I always do' was my only response, but I thought to myself that the next day I would listen to the evening news only once. And I really meant it, but when the last stroke of seven sounded, I went to the radio as usual and switched it on. Why shouldn't I listen if I want to, I thought; and what I had previously done unconsciously for heaven knows how long, I now began to do deliberately.

"In the mornings I got up early to hear the first bulletin, and I often arrived late for work because I didn't want to miss the last of the eight o'clock news. The management threatened to sack me, but I didn't mind. I wanted to be sacked, because my office was in the city center and I couldn't go home for lunch, so I always missed the one o'clock news." He fell silent, and I saw him through a chink in the curtain. His eyebrows, greasy blond tufts under a cloth forehead, and the sagging purplish eyelids above the bulging cheeks, formed a protective ring around the weak, withdrawn gray eyes. When I asked, "Is that all?" the mouth, droopy and vague, began to speak again.

"No," he said, "but I don't think you understand. I don't think another person can understand that I was glad when I was sacked, free to construct a ritual around my myth: the voice. I saved up for a beautiful chair, and having bought one, I placed it right in front of the radio. I listened to the news with the lights out; a candle made it more wonderful. How happy I was! The voice swept over me and stood behind me, beside me, close to me. Here I am, said the voice, here I am, and it touched me and took me with it and caressed me and filled the room until there was almost total darkness and I no longer heard the words but floated on them, on the sound, as if in a little boat without destination. It was my room, mine, in which the voice fanned out like a fragrance.

"I know now that I was probably close to going crazy. But then? At night I dreamed of the voice, but they weren't happy dreams. I saw myself sleeping in a room of which I was the white, radiant center. Around me moved a bluish, breathing light. Because the dream was always the same, I knew that at a given moment this light would stand still and become immobile, stop breathing, and then fall apart on the floor into sharp, blue-black dust. Shining white and unassailable, I remained the center of the room until the dust was trodden. For although nothing became visible, the center suddenly shifted away from me to the place where the dust was being trodden. It began to my right, at the back of the room, and slowly moved toward me, and although I haven't, or rather hadn't, really the slightest tangible evidence, I believed the voice to be in the room from the moment the sound of the dust became audible. At the same time a chain of sharp, oblong stones began to form around my neck. They were black stones—at least they were at first—but the color slowly drew away from them and began to blend with the white of my face. Then there occurred an irrevocable division, for below the chain the body remained immobile and dazzlingly white, but above it, the face was alive, like a hideous gray mask, an embryonic earth, trembling and shaking and then slowly bursting open.

"I bent forward and looked into a long street of tall houses built of bricks of an enchanting, tender green color. But I could never, never enter that street. Each time I tried, a hateful barrier formed, a barricade consisting of a bluish powder that bit me and wounded me. If I nevertheless pressed on, the powder piled up higher and higher and became more vicious, so that it became impossible even to see the street. I don't think I woke up immediately after the dream; I think that my dream vanished gradually. During the daytime I was never in the least troubled by it, because then the announcer's voice was there again, and I was busy with the preparations for listening.

"Until that particular night. The dream ran its usual course. I was there, gleaming, apparently unassailable; the light breathed and froze as before; the dust came and was trampled. Everything was normal. The chain laid itself around my neck, and my face became hideously discolored and distorted again. It burst open, and through the repulsive wound the street appeared, delightful as always, and as always I tried to enter it. But the attempt had been reduced to a ritual gesture, for I hadn't truly tried it for a long time, afraid as I was of the sharpness of the dust that hit back at me viciously with the first step I took. This time, though, there was no dust, and I was able to walk into the street. I was afraid. Obtaining something you have wanted for a long time makes you frightened at first.

"Apart from the green color of the houses, this was the ordinary world, and yet it was pervaded with an indefinable tenderness that silently wiped out my fear and gave way to a feeling of ecstatic rapture instead. I began to sing, I bought flowers somewhere, and suddenly I realized that this was no ordinary town. This is the face of things when you are happy, I thought. The world is always like this. We paint it with our own colors of fear or unhappiness, but really the world is always like this. That is why"—his voice hesitated behind the curtains—"that is why it is so difficult to describe the world. It would mean describing oneself, for the world adopts the colors we give to it.

"I wondered why I should be happy in this world. The houses were tall and narrow, and some had window boxes full of marigolds and geraniums; but that is so in all cities. Gradually the streets became narrower and the houses lower and older. And then I met the bird of paradise. 'Hello Janet,' I said. But Janet looked at me indifferently with her two dead beads. (Children were playing on that street, and a man was playing music for money; but that is also the same in all cities.) 'How long have you been standing in this window?' I asked. 'You have become a bit dustier, but then it is a long time since Mary Jane and I solemnly plighted our troth to each other in front of this store, with you and all Mr. Lace's other stuffed animals as our witnesses. Till death do us part. Oh, Janet,' I said, 'don't look so dead. You were our friend after all, the concluder of our pacts, the patient, silent witness to our evening monologues. Here in your presence Mary Jane and I first met each other, when we stood with our noses flattened against the windowpane, watching Mr. Lace putting you on display. "It's so mean," said Mary Jane. "Yes," I agreed. "Shall we buy it?" And we decided to buy you, and entered the store. I remembered the dry, breathless air, the clang of the doorbell, and then the quick little footsteps of Mr. Lace. But you were not for sale, said the voice amid the folds and wrinkles; you were very rare and therefore very expensive. We possessed only seven shillings between us, and thus founded a society, Mary Jane and I: the SLJ, the Society for the Liberation of Janet.'

" 'I still have the kitty,' said Mary Jane behind me. 'Twenty-three shillings and sixpence?' I asked, and she nodded that it was so. 'You have grown beautiful,' I said, because I could see her reflection in the window, 'and your dress is beautiful, too.' I turned and kissed her on the forehead. She laughed. 'I made it out of the cloth of old lampshades.' 'It's lovely,' I said, and then I shook hands with her and gave her the flowers I had bought. 'Hi, Janet,' we said. 'We've come to collect you.' The bell clanged as before, just as we had thought it would, and the dry, breathless air still lived there. 'No,' said Mr. Lace, 'I can't sell this bird. I am keeping it for two young children nearby, who are saving up for it.' 'That's us, Mr. Lace. We have grown up,' whispered Mary Jane.

" 'Oh, I see,' he said, 'I see,' and he carefully lifted Janet out of the display case and brushed the dust off her with his little hands of weathered marble. Then he clasped his hands around the bird's neck, like some superfluous Victorian ornamentation. 'You must be careful with it.' His voice leaped with a strange little wail that bounced against the dusty silence of the animals. 'You'd better go now,' he said, and withdrew his hands with a jerk, as though they had been stuck to the bird.

" 'What time is it?' I asked her. 'It's evening,' she said, and we walked to the nearby gardens. I carried the bird of paradise called Janet on my left arm. 'Why did you never come back? Why did you never write?' she asked. 'Don't ask,' I said. 'Don't ask anything.'

" 'The Reverend Thubbs died today,' she said, and as I did

not reply, she thought perhaps that I did not care, but she continued. "He was the assistant preacher, long ago. Don't you remember you used to go to services in other districts if you knew he was preaching there? I was so jealous of him because I thought you loved him better than me. When he preached, I saw you sitting there, from where I sat in the girls' pew, but you never looked at me. It was as if you didn't even belong to the other boys any longer, but sat among them like a stranger, someone to whom something special was happening.' 'Is he dead?' I asked. She nodded, and that was the end of my dream.

"I saw her growing blurred and faint, while the curves and graceful contours of her alabaster face reappeared briefly above the faded orange-red of her dress. She receded from me like a small sad statue, holding, as pointless ornaments, a bunch of flowers and a stuffed bird of paradise.

"Waking up was different this time. I was not happy; I didn't even put the chair by the radio. It wasn't so much the memory of the dream that oppressed me and cast a shadow on me, as the realization that a mistake had been made somewhere. This feeling remained, for when the announcer was later killed in a car crash, I still felt, days after he had been buried, that a mistake had been made somewhere.

"I now dreamed of Mary Jane at night, but without the usual preliminaries. It had become easy to enter our street and stand by the window of Mr. Lace's store. She would join me there with Janet under her arm, and then we would go for a walk. 'The Reverend Thubbs will be buried tomorrow,' she said on the second day; and later, on another day, 'The Reverend Thubbs was buried today. I was at the funeral.' The houses, green and motionless, listened, though perhaps not really to us; houses know about these things, after all. She wore her faded dresses of delicate orange-red silk and buried the Reverend Thubbs every day anew, while the wind blew her hair about and ruffled Janet's feathers as though it all concerned something quite different.

"There were evenings enough, in that city. Somewhat timidly they alighted, filling everything with a friendly darkness in which Mary Jane could say, 'Today it is a week ago that the Reverend Thubbs was buried. Did you know records were made of him? Somewhere far away is his voice, as buried as the Reverend Thubbs himself. Isn't it strange, the voice of the Reverend Thubbs on a round, black disc?' 'No,' I said, 'I don't think that's strange,' and when I woke up that day, I decided to go to the street where I used to live and where Mr. Lace's store must still be. Perhaps I should have gone there earlier?

"The street was far away and hard to find, because it was so long ago. The houses are not green, I thought; and indeed it was painful, for they were dirty and not even melancholy. It was a street of poverty in which the curtains concealed comfortless interiors. Children played in it, because children always play everywhere, but it was a game of snatching and snatching back, amid raucous cries. 'Do you know Mr. Lace's store?' I asked a boy. 'No,' he said, 'there is no Mr. Lace around here.' The other children gathered around. 'There is no Mr. Lace around here.' 'It was a corner store,' I said. No, there was no Mr. Lace on the corner. 'What kind of store was it?' the children asked. 'It had dead birds in the window.' 'There is a store here that has one dead bird in the window, at the end of the last block.'

"I went there and saw Janet, lonely and a little ridiculous, perched amid common grocer's wares. 'Hi, stranger,' her voice said behind me, and though it was not the voice from the dream, I knew it must be her. 'Hi,' I said. 'Why have you changed your clothes?' 'Changed my clothes? What do you mean? What kind of a joker are you?' She did not recognize me, and if I had not seen her in my dreams, I might not have recognized her either. She had changed her clothes and was the same height as me, for the soles of her shoes were thick and the heels too high. To cover the first signs of decline she had put on too much makeup, and her hair hung in wet locks on her forehead.

" 'Have you any money, stranger?' she asked. 'Yes,' I said, 'let's go in.' The man behind the counter greeted us but looked at her mockingly. 'What can I do for you?' 'That bird. I would like to buy that bird.' He looked at me. 'I've waited a long time for this,' he said. 'When I took over the business from Mr. Lace, ten years ago, he asked me to keep that bird in the window, because two children who lived near here were saving up for it. These children were sure to come for it some day, and here they are. One of them I know, I may say'—'Shut up,' she said behind me—'and the other one I do not know. Actually,' he continued in his thin, unperturbed voice, 'I am rather attached to that bird.' 'Here's the money,' I said. 'Hurry up.' He drawled, 'Oh, we're in a hurry, are we,' but he took Janet from the window and placed her on the counter. 'Stupid corpse,' he said, and hit her so that the dust blew up.

"I looked at Mary Jane. 'I've bought her,' I said. 'I've bought Janet. It may be a bit late, but I have bought her.' She asked, 'How many times must you look before you understand things?' Two times, I thought—the first time and now. I saw her pulling the bird from the counter by the legs. 'Damn you,' she swore, 'there you go!' It was as if Janet screamed as she fell between us. The head broke off and rolled away from the protruding, hideous innards of decayed, stinking hay. Deader than ever, the macabre stiff legs on the wooden mount stuck into the air amid the dust that rose up as though in a miniature bomb explosion. 'Get out,' said Mary Jane, and I was aware of the two of them standing behind me like two figures from some sinister mime. The bell clanged when I opened the door and left. 'Did you find it?' asked the children. 'Yes,' I said, 'I found it.'

"I had indeed found it. And then it may happen that you start hitchhiking. Who knows, in Germany you might meet a boy who asks, 'Have you seen a girl with a Chinese face?' And why shouldn't you then go on looking together—it is a goal, is it not? And then you sometimes sit here behind a curtain and you tell your story, always the same story, all over again to someone who doesn't even listen."

"I did listen," I said. "I heard it all. I want to go outside."

As I went out of the door, I caught sight of the room as if it were in a picture—the three of them standing there with the beatific impersonality of primitive statues, representing nostalgia, sorrow, longing. I hurried down the stairs and went into the garden. It was no longer raining, but there was a noisy wind that made the trees bow like drunken ladies-in-waiting as, laughing uncontrollably, it swept the clouds across the sky.

I heard them telling their stories again; I saw them again, moving their hands to the rhythms of their memories. Perhaps it was loneliness that invaded them like flies invade a carcass. I know nothing about that, though I think that the loneliness people talk so much about can't be the real loneliness, and that one day a loneliness will come that marks people, not with the sign of Cain, but with a sign that proves their humanity. We have not yet become used to it, I think. Perhaps the time we live in now is only a prelude to real loneliness.

No, it was no longer raining, but because it was so windy, I did not hear Heinz approach.

"Do you know the *Agony of Christ* by Geertgen tot Sint Jans?" he asked.

"Why have you come here?" I asked. "I wanted to be here. I didn't want to talk to you. Why have you come?"

"Do you know the *Agony of Christ* by Geertgen tot Sint Jans?" he asked again.

"No," I said, "I don't."

"It's going to rain," he said. "You must come on to the verandah."

"Why? I want to stay in the rain."

"Otherwise you can't see the *Agony of Christ*."

We went to the verandah, to the point where the light from the upper window cast a faint beam below.

"Look," he said, "the *Agony of Christ*," and between his thin, chalky, dry hands he held a small reproduction. It was a photograph cut out of a magazine, glued onto cardboard.

"It's crumpled," I said. "It's dirty. I can hardly see it."

"There's little left of it," he replied. "I always carry it with me. Have done so for years. It is my denial. Look closely."

It showed a standing Christ figure, a man with his body gashed open. With a pitiful, childish gesture he tries to stop the blood that pours from his side. The pain on the faces of the man, his mother, and his friend John is cruelly emphasized, underscored by the cross that, dark and brutal, slants across the picture. Angels with small, sorrowful faces, carrying the attributes of suffering, fill the space that is overcrowded and oppressive and that creates a suffocation visible around the staring eyes of the tormented man.

"You see?" asked Heinz. "This is my denial. Denial, just like their soberness, their serenity if you like."

"What do you mean, theirs?" I asked.

"The other monks, those who were there because they had a vocation, not because they wanted to belong together as I did, not because of the appeal of the liturgy, but because of what is behind it. Not, therefore, like me, enchanted and spellbound by the wonderful wisdom of the psalms, and even more by their nostalgic intonations; not by garments and gestures, but by this and this and this"—and he pointed at the wounds of the man in the picture as if he were inflicting them again, savagely.

He continued. "To me he was a man who, though innocent, was beaten and crucified like many others in those days. A saint, perhaps; a prophet, perhaps—but a god? His divinity haunted me all those years because they believed in it. That was why I had no right to be there. Maybe as a doubter, but I wasn't even that. To me he remained the man with the wounds, the man full of reproach in his agony. To them he was the man who had called them. Oh yes, I knew what was behind those faces I constantly saw around me, grave and demure as in primitive pictures. Christ the man, the mediator by virtue of the hypostatic union and therefore offering the sacrifice of his life to God to atone for the sins of mankind—here in this picture, suffering. And they, continuing this sacrifice as priests, derived their priesthood from his high-priesthood, but also experienced an everlasting Agony of Christ.

"Do you understand? I was jealous. If I had been able to, I would have hated them. Hated, not because they, like me, got up at two o'clock in the morning. Not because they, like me, ate dry bread, and never any meat, fish, or eggs. Not because they were silent, like me, and felt cold in the corridors and exhaustion from working on the land. No, but because they had a reason outside themselves to do all these things, and I didn't. That is why. Perhaps it sounds strange, but in principle they were always outside themselves, and I never was. I told you I had to leave as soon as I started having seizures. I had no vocation, they said, and they were doubly right, though they did not know it. Right because the *canon* demands both inner and outward fitness. I hid my inner unfitness. I denied it, forgive me. But my outward unfitness was obvious, and in matters of physical soundness a very strict logic is followed. If someone is not of sound body, he is outwardly unfit; ergo, he has not been called by God. Priests with only one hand are not called by God, priests with epilepsy are not called by God. This must be far worse for people who think they have a true vocation, unlike someone like me, a hanger-on, ridiculous in my own eyes. Well, as far as physical fitness is concerned, I don't blame them. If times had been normal, I would have had a medical test before I ever entered."

He was silent, and we listened to the groaning of the house under the passionate caresses of the wind, and then he said, "Because finally, my friend, a priest is merely a utensil."

4

The next day was a quiet day. We were there but we did not speak, and later on I left. I saw them sleeping. Their faces were wonderfully empty after the stories of the previous night. Sargon's soft pink hand lay on Heinz's shoulder. He looked a bit big and clumsy, like a baroque angel fallen from an altar and suddenly grown in size. He woke up and sought me with his eyes.

"You were looking at me," he said.

"Yes," I replied.

"Do you think life is short?" he asked. When I answered that I did not know, he said that he was sure it wasn't short but, on the contrary, immensely long and that he always thought of that when he woke up. "Take him," he pointed. "We have been together for more than a year now. Life is as short as grass, he always says, but that is not true. Here, these thin hands and this white, sick face that already looks so old, I've known them for such a long time already. And do you think I would know them if I hadn't seen them for so long? I know him the way a child knows the road he takes to school every day—that tree and that house and those old people sitting in the front window eating. And here, that stain on his right hand, the dryness of his skin and the oldness in his voice. It is as if I had spent one life with myself and one with him. You collect so many lives in the long run that they seem to sit on your shoulders and press down and stifle you until you start talking in order to get rid of them. But they stay nevertheless and slowly put their mark on you. They mark their weight and their oppressiveness on your face, on your hands—have you seen how ugly I am? These people who say that a year passes quickly forget that they would need another year to recount all that has happened in the one that has gone. I am going to sleep."

He lay down again, with his eyes closed. His eyelids lay like patches of tired violet on the paleness of his skin, and a moment later he was asleep, for he smacked his lips the way some people do when they sleep, or children.

What have I to do with these people, I wondered. It was as if they had come from another world, a strange land, for as they slept they became distant from me, moving farther and farther away. I thought of leaving them and going in search of the Chinese girl, because I had seen her in Calais, because she hadn't stopped when I called her in the rain, because I had searched for her then, in Calais, and in all those other places for no other reason than that I wanted to talk to her. But when I had packed my rucksack, Fay said, "You mustn't go yet. Let them leave first. I want you to stay a bit longer."

"You were asleep," I said, but she replied that she hadn't been asleep and that she didn't want me to leave.

"I have to pick flowers again tomorrow and you must help me."

"I'll come back," I said. "I will come back. I'll leave my rucksack here." And I left for the city of Luxembourg.

The trains that arrive there enter by a rail bridge in the form of a tall, graceful Roman aqueduct. It was evening when I walked beneath this bridge to Les Trois Glands, a high point from which you can see very far. But it was dark now, and the valley was an immense bowl of silence, sometimes startled by nocturnal sounds—water perhaps, or the moon talking. I was unable to sit down, for all the benches were occupied by people who loved each other or who at least made the sorts of movements to suggest they did.

I know these parks. It isn't difficult to know them, for you always walk on the same gravelly soil that crunches under your soles. All parks join one to another—the Slotterspark in Oslo, the Luxembourg in Paris, the Vondelpark in Amsterdam, and the Villa Borghese in Rome. You walk down a very long path lined on both sides with benches on which people sit. They are the chorus—the chorus of people seated on park benches and of a boy walking down the path in the middle.

"Why do you disturb us," they say. "This was our evening. It was specially prepared for us with silence, with trees possibly rustling with secrets. This was our evening; the moon is regally up and walks wistfully through the fragrances of trees and earth, touching the fragrance of our bodies; and somewhere—where?—water is seeping."

"Why do you say that?" I ask.

They: Can't you see how we suddenly stiffen when you approach? You are the intruder, the unwelcome one.

I: Why do you cling to that which you should let go of? For your caresses are mortal; you cannot hold the spell.

They: And when you pass by we sit rigidly like stone, and often we look ridiculous as we sit there. You have intruded upon us. You are a crowd.

I: Soon you will leave together, and maybe you will sleep together if you have not already done so here. And you will wake up tomorrow morning. Yes, one of you will wake before the other and see what he or she loves or does not love, what he has caressed with hands and mouth. It will be seen in the light, and it will be strange, as if magnified. It will suddenly be frightening, a strange body close by.

They: And when you have gone past, you hear, odiously, odiously, the shifting of a foot on the path, a foot bracing itself so that the body may the better bend forward.

I: I pass between you in all the parks of the world. I walk past love, and I do not understand it. You cannot divide yourself, surely. In the morning, when it is time to go to work, you leave each other, and the bodies begin their lonely journey, both the caressed body and mine, the uncaressed one. They move farther away from each other than the night can ever reconcile or reunite.

They: What can you do? We know our imperfection, but

one loves not because of pity for one's own mortality. The one we have here with us is the only one. We hold this only one in the evening light, and she is a secret; we hold her in the light of her secret, and she becomes enveloped in tenderness.

I: And this only one, if you had not met her then and there, you would have had to find another only one, for the world is full of only ones because they must be found.

They: An only one is never found; she arises. Her gestures reveal her, and she arises from what she says and what we hear her say. She acquires shape as a result of the occasion she gives and the opportunities we give her to give occasion. What we caress and hold is what we have encountered then and there; but what we comprehend of it, we have made.

I: If I walk on and on in the evening—which has for me, too, arrayed itself in glory, which puts its hands on the day's restlessness and on my troubled thoughts—if I walk on, and if I should find a seat, and if I were to sit on it with another, would I not lose myself?

They: That would be impossible. You do not lose yourself unless it be in your own inadequacy. What you are afraid of is imitation, of imitating us and our gestures. But that is impossible; everyone has his own gesture, his own words, and his own smell, like a code number. You do not walk here in pride but in fear, and it is not good to walk here among us and break what we have built here this evening, like bits of firewood, on the hardness of your doubts. We have little time. Another day, as we walk here, and it will seem to us as if our blood has run dry; the bodies by which we have known each other will begin the treason of old age, rubbing our memories to dust against a hard dryness.

I: What then is the difference, in the end?

They: That one does not live in the end; one lives now. Now, with the tensions of a body and the subtlety of a hand stroking it; now, with the secret language of a mouth and the longing of another mouth meeting it.

Yes, I said, yes.

Fay was waiting for me when I arrived at her house. "Have

they gone?" I asked. But they hadn't gone yet, the others. We sat down on the verandah, and she put an arm around my shoulders. But then she said, "No, on the wall," and we walked to the wall. She climbed up first and pulled me up. We sat on the wall, facing the water. I think we must have sat there for a long time, she with her arm heavily around my shoulders, from time to time passing her broad hand with the red nails across my mouth. Later I put my arm around her shoulders, too, the way I did when walking with my school friends and telling each other secrets.

"Hi, Fay," I said, and she laughed. I asked, "Isn't it strange to be so beautiful?"

"Strange?"

"Yes," I said, and I cautiously put my hand on her breast. "You are beautiful; I think that must be strange. It's different for *things* to be beautiful, but if a woman is beautiful, she knows it. That is very different."

"You don't love me, do you?" she said.

"I don't know," I said. "I don't think so, but I can't tell, because I've never done it before."

"You love her, I think," she said.

I don't know, I thought. I only want to talk to her.

"Philip," Fay started again.

"Yes?"

"Do you think I'm too old to play ball?"

"No," I said, "I don't think so."

"Sometimes, when there is no one here, I play ball on my own. I run across the yard and bounce it—I count how many times—and sometimes I throw it up against the wall and catch it again. I have had that ball for a long time, but these days I use it only when I am sure no one can see me."

"I don't mind playing with you," I said. "It isn't so long ago since I last played ball."

We got down from the wall and she put her hand on my neck again, as she had done that time by the lilacs.

"You don't think I'm too old to play ball?" she asked again.

"No," I replied.

"Only children play ball, surely?"

"Children, too."

She pressed her nails deeper. Don't bite, I thought, but she said, "We can't see; it's too dark. The ball will get lost and then we won't be able to find it."

"Go and get it," I said. "We can see well enough in the moonlight."

"Yes, there's always the moon."

She tipped her head back and looked at me with her eyes half-closed. "I've slept with lots of men."

"I know," I said.

"I've never played ball with a boy since."

"Go and get it then."

And she nodded and went to the house to get the ball. It was a large blue ball with yellow stripes, and we played among the stones while the others slept. We did not speak, and we threw the ball to each other as hard as possible. Later we had a competition and she won, for she was as lithe as an animal. It was almost like a dance when she jumped to catch the ball or bent backward to throw it. Once she came toward me with the ball in her hands. "I think this ball is happiness," she said. "I must catch it every time, but you must throw it as hard as you can."

When she went back to her place I threw the ball high and far to the moon, so that for a moment it glittered coldly and dangerously. "Here is your happiness!" I called, "Catch it!" and she leaped toward it like a large, desperate bird, her arms like gleaming wings in which she clutched the ball as she fell. "Are you hurt?" I asked, but she said merely, "I've got it," and we went on playing, perhaps for hours. Afterward we slept on the verandah, for it wasn't cold that night.

When I woke from the sound of the others coming down the stairs, I saw that Fay was still asleep with her right arm stretched out in a curve, as if someone were there or as if beckoning, and her left hand was on the ball, which lay between us, innocently blue and yellow in the light of the day.

Heinz spread out a large map of Europe on the floor, and with a red pencil he drew a line from Plymouth via Paris and

Zürich to Trieste. "What's that?" I asked, but he marked the part of Europe above the line with a *1* and below the line with a *2*. So *1* was England, northern France, the Netherlands, Belgium, Luxembourg, and Scandinavia, and *2* was France, Spain, Portugal, Switzerland, Italy, and Yugoslavia. "Tactics," he said. "It's simply a question of tactics. You are *1* and we are *2;* you search in *1,* we search in *2.*" No, I thought, I shall search where I like. But I didn't mind going there, so I said I agreed.

Heinz's rucksack was a collapsed, flat object, a quixotic attribute peculiarly in keeping with the bearer. He ran the tip of his tongue over his dry lips and said, "Goodbye, my friend," and then he made a movement of his hands as if he wanted to add something or do something, but he didn't, and slowly, as though his burden were heavy, he walked down the driveway. He turned once, to see if Sargon was coming, and he was as pale as the morning.

"Are you coming, Sargon?" he asked.

"I have to tell him something first," called Sargon.

"No," I said, "I no longer belong to you. I am 1, you are 2. He decided it. I don't have to belong anymore."

But he took me by the arm and pulled me gently along. "Up to the main road?" he asked. All the way to the main road the wide pinkish mouth and the eyes nearly hidden in the bloated gray face told me about Sargon—that he had written poetry but had given it up in the end because all he had ever found on the paper was himself, himself in disarray. "I tried philosophy," he said, and so he went on talking. I heard about Thomas Aquinas and the five proofs of the existence of God. Of course, that was the answer, he thought; it all fitted. But Schopenhauer's simplistic denial of a Creator had confused him. All the philosophers had confused him and made him feel uncertain because of their conflicting certainties—utterly uncertain, for although he had got no further than popular digests of their works, the quotations these contained had made an impression on him that he regarded as the aroma of truth.

"I gave it up," he said.

"Sargon," called Heinz. He was now far ahead of us.

"You'd better go back now," said Sargon. We said goodbye to each other and I went back to Fay.

"They've gone," I said, and she said I should leave as well. I fetched my rucksack from upstairs, but when I went down again, she wasn't there to say goodbye. Maybe she had climbed over the wall and was now picking flowers on the other side, or playing ball. I didn't know, so I left, and because I was *1* I went north.

In the land of Meuse and Waal I got a job in the cherry harvest because I had run out of money. We went around the orchards, chasing away the starlings with a rattle. Hoooo-woooo-woooo-woooo, we shouted, and we rattled and beat on tin cans. When the cherry picking was over, I went to the isle of Texel to gather foliage and later to dig flower bulbs. I do not remember very much of it; the ground was wet in the morning, and dry and painful in the afternoon when the sun stood high. Kneeling on the ground, we dug up bulbs with our hands, afterward placing them in large sieves and shaking them so that the lumps of earth were knocked off them. And I remember that it rained sometimes and that we bent over the vastness of the field, as if we were caressing the earth, longing to return into it. For although it is perhaps not true, many of us have a feeling of having been born from the earth rather than from a woman.

I did these things to earn money, for I wanted to go on searching for her, and I did, in the Netherlands and then in Germany, but I did not find her. And so September came, and early one morning I crossed the frontier into Denmark.

After going through passport control I looked at the stamp and saw KRUSAA, Inrejst. I looked around, and she was really there.

5

Anyone who now goes through the passport control at Krusaa can perhaps still see me, for I am standing to the right of the road by the bushes, saying to her, "Hello, I've been looking for you everywhere."

She was now wearing a black velvet jacket above her tight-fitting cord pants, and little girl's shoes with straps on her bare feet.

"Aren't you cold?" I asked. "Bare feet? It's already fall here."

"Yes," she said. "We'll buy some socks in Copenhagen."

"Maybe we'll find some sooner if we don't get a lift all the way to Copenhagen. But you can wear some of mine till then."

So she did, for my feet were not much bigger than hers, and we set off along the road. In her left hand she carried two slim, flat cases. She tied together their handles with shoelaces so that she could carry them more easily. Over her right arm hung a bag of clothes and food.

Our first lift took us to Aabenraa, and there we bought socks and played cards in a café. "I'm only going as far as Haderslev," said the next driver, but he took us all the way to Copenhagen. We couldn't imagine why, for he didn't speak to us. It was still afternoon when he picked us up and night when he dropped us on the outskirts of Copenhagen. Because he didn't talk, we didn't either; she spoke to me again on the ferry, after he had left us. We leaned over the rail at the stern, looking at the wake and at the lights flicking on in Nyborg.

"What do you like doing?" she asked.

"I like reading and looking at pictures and riding on a bus in the evening or at night, like when I'm celebrating with my uncle Antonin Alexander."

"And what else?"

"Sitting by the water," I said, "and walking in the rain and sometimes kissing someone. And you?"

She reflected and then said, "Singing in the street, or sitting by the roadside and talking to myself, or crying because it is going to rain. But you can't really do any of those things; you can't sit by the roadside talking to yourself, because people will think you're crazy, so you have to go away."

"What else do you like doing?"

"Thinking I am like my grandmother."

What is your grandmother like? I wondered, but before I could ask, she told me: "Sometimes she is strange to me, because living alone makes it hard for her to be with children."

You don't even have a grandmother at all, I thought. It isn't true, or Maventer would have told me.

"She is old now, and very straight, and usually she is angry with us children. We wonder why. I think it is very sad, because everyone condemns the way she lives. No one understands that she is a wild soul that lives and suffers in a corner, where it will die. I think she is most like the month of November. They've told me that her legs are sore all over and covered in scratches from the roots and thorns and tree stumps in the woods where she goes for walks for hours on end. She always goes alone with a sickle in her hand. I followed her once or twice. She is like an animal, a wild animal looking for a spot to die alone."

I guessed that this was the picture she had imagined of herself when she had grown old, though I wasn't sure. The water foamed beneath us, and we watched it play with the moon, which tried to keep up with the ship. But it was later in the night, in the city, that our game was born, because, as it was so late, we didn't bother going to bed. We took a tram till we came to water, at a place called Nyhavn.

"There's a little boat," she said. We left our baggage on the quayside and sat down in the boat.

"What's your name?" I asked. I knew she was called Marcelle because Maventer had told me.

"You have to make up a name for me," she said, and she turned to me so swiftly that the boat rocked. The old ivory of her face became strange and immobile before my eyes.

"You're so close now," I whispered. "May I hold your face?" As she did not reply, I put my hands around her face. They were made for that; the shape of her cheekbones grew in the palms of my hands. "Close your eyes," I said. I wanted to kiss her on the eyelids that closed tremblingly over her eyes, purple like those flowers you sometimes see by the side of marshes in the South, of which I cannot remember the name. "I'll call you Champignon," I said, and then I let go of her carefully, afraid that it would hurt my hands and her face. She laughed and her face was suffused with loveliness. The light played on her teeth and hid and chased itself under her eyes, which were large and still incomprehensible.

"What's in those suitcases?" I asked, thinking she might not want to tell me, since she hadn't told me her name. But she untied the shoelaces and opened the cases.

"This is my retinue," she said. "I am going to hold court." And then she became a princess. It was a small record player with records. "And this is also my retinue," she said, pointing to a little book that stuck out above the edge of her jacket. "Shall I call them?"

Yes, I thought, and I said, "Yes, why not."

"But then you'll have to call yours."

I have no retinue, I wanted to say, but I thought of all the things Maventer had told me about her, and I replied, "I think I'll call mine, too; I think I will."

"You have a book, too, haven't you?"

"Yes," I admitted, for although most people find it strange if you read poetry, I thought she would perhaps not laugh. I showed her the little book I always carried and in which I wrote down my favorite poems.

"Good," she nodded. "It's like mine, a good retinue, a very noble cortege. Do you have a comb?"

I gave her my comb, and she combed her hair and smoothed her clothes and told me I should do the same.

"Why?" I asked, but she did not answer and wanted to know where we were.

"In a rowboat," I said, "in the Nyhavn, Copenhagen."

"Yes," she said as if she thought this was very important, "and now that we have combed our hair, I think we are ready to receive our courtiers."

She put on a record, the cortège from a sonata by Domenico Scarlatti. It was a fantastic sight, then, to see three boats decorated with asters and scabious sailing up from the Havngade. In the first boat, which was beflagged in autumnal colors, the chamber orchestra sat motionlessly, though perhaps the silver of a wig stirred under the light, or the lace of a frill. But that was not important; they all sat like statues while the harpsichordist played the cortège.

"It is Scarlatti himself," she whispered, and I remembered that this was the man who sometimes visited my uncle Antonin Alexander, and to whom I had once been introduced without having seen him. "Are the others there, too?" I asked her. But only those composers whose records she had were there. "That one with the red hair, behind there, that is Vivaldi," she pointed, and I saw her blush briefly when he bowed toward her.

The boats came alongside. "If we look in our books, you'll recognize them," she said. "Look." She laid her little book open in her lap. I saw the men talking quietly to one another, and noticed that some were wearing costumes from long bygone and forgotten times, that some were old and very tired, and that, really, all their faces had an air of oldness about them.

"There is Paul Eluard," she nudged me. I saw him and

whispered, "Why is he here?" She pointed in her book, and for a moment the wind did not hide the light with clouds, so that I saw the lines:

> avec tes yeux, je change comme avec les lunes

and

> Pourquois suis-je si belle?
> Parceque mon maître me lave.

He shook hands with us and sat and talked with us for a while. In this same way I talked to many people that evening, for I introduced those from my retinue to her, such as e. e. cummings, because he wrote the poem that goes, "somewhere I never travelled, gladly beyond any experience, your eyes have their silence," and because the poem ends with "the voice of your eyes is deeper than all the roses, nobody, not even the rain, has such small hands."

And there were others from my book, like Becquer, from Spain—"I am protecting a treasure from love." And from hers, "because our countries are too far apart." With the man who had written that, she spoke in the language I had heard in the village near Chez Sylvestre, and from his dress I understood he must be a troubadour. It was Jaufre Rudel, and with him were Arnaut Daniel and Bernard de Ventadour.

On that weird evening, the city was silent behind us, and when the orchestra was not playing, the men talked in the three boats that lay like a horseshoe around our rowboat. To the soft music Hans Lodeizen said,

> I live in another house
> sometimes we meet
> I always sleep without you
> and we are always together.

And even Paul van Ostayen had come, with his Harlequin in water green and Columbine in faded pink, from the insignificant little polka.

So she held court that night in the Nyhavn, and toward

morning, when the city began to grow pale, the boats sailed away and we walked back along the water, back to the people. Yet I did not tell her that I loved her until perhaps a week later, for by then I had seen her in sun and in rain, belonging to some sea breeze or other, or talking softly in the early morning cold when we had not been to sleep. I had seen her at night, in the sultry warmth of a truck on the roads in Sweden, asleep on my shoulder, and we knew each other because we were together, sailing away from Elsinore with Hamlet's castle behind us, and sleeping in the forests by Lake Varna, where the nights are mysterious with old age and we suspected Loki's wrath behind sinister shadows.

So I told her in Stockholm. And who knows, I might not have told her even then if it hadn't been raining, for I did not think she could love me, and in that case it ought to be left unsaid. But it was raining, and because we always sought the water, we were lying under a bridge, the Kungsbron, sheltered from the rain in a hollow between the road and the slow arch on which the bridge rests.

Cars drove overhead and I said, "I love you." But she opened her eyes, she sought my face and stroked it briefly before replying—if it can be called a reply—"Of course."

Then we lay still for a very long time, until she began to talk again.

"Did you know I am leaving?"

"No," I said, "I didn't know," and I knew I was going to lose this game because I loved her, because we fitted into each other like two hands; and yet she was going away.

"Did you know," she asked, "that life is a lovely thing?" and before I was able to reply she spoke again. "You will go on looking for the smallest certainties, I think, and you will go on becoming attached to people and to places, and most of all you will go on finding the world lovely, because you always have. I do, too, though I hardly know who I am, and certainly not why I am here. Maybe I exist only to wonder and to look at people and see that life is its own comfort, although I think you can see that only when you believe that this world is the worst possible world, hopeless and sad and doomed to perish, yet for that reason amazing, arousing tenderness, and most of all, lovely."

She fell silent and I lifted her slightly so that she could lie in the crook of my arm. The rain was still falling and bloomed in front of the hollow like pictures in a window. I reflected that the loveliness of the world begins anew with each new person, that it cannot be explained, and that, as my uncle Antonin Alexander said, "a paradise lives beside it." And I saw that we, too, are amazing and arouse tenderness, because we are fragile, failed gods, doomed from the start, each one of us. But we can always pretend; everyone can pretend.

It was strange loving her—strange loving anyone, since I had never done it before. I noticed everything about her—about her face, which I sometimes felt with my hands as if I were creating it anew; about the things she said and did not say; about the way she prepared herself to hold court, combing her hair and painting her lips with a little brush. She did it as earnestly as a child playing with grown-ups' things. The last gesture of the ritual was always that I brushed the soft skin behind her ears with Ma Griffe perfume.

The next day we sat by the Saltsjön under the heavy oak trees of Djurgarden, watching the ships sailing to and from the Baltic Sea. Crows screeched above us, loudly announcing the coming of winter, for it was autumn everywhere, especially in the countryside in the following days, when we traveled north

Now I would have to lose her, the evening of a storm. We had traveled through Lapland and down again along the Norwegian coast until we came to Nordfjord. The mountains, squatting like mighty animals near the mouth of the fjord, thundered and roared with the storm, and we heard the water howl and bellow. The rain lashed us, and holding onto each other, we ran to a barn we had seen from the road.

I switched on my flashlight and saw her looking at me, and I noticed for the first time the color of red jasper in her eyes.

She looked at me in the way she had looked at me once when she was not feeling well, in the North, near Abisko. "Are you ill?" I had asked her, "or are you merely sad?" She had laughed and replied, "Girls have these spells every month, you know."

This time she said, "We are sad."

"Yes, because you are going away."

We were standing apart, and she came toward me. I caught her and laid her down and kissed her. I held her as if this could prevent her from going away, for I knew she would go away, I knew it—that I had searched for her and found her, that she belonged to me, and that she would nonetheless go away, alone. She stroked my back as I held her in my arms. I took her hair between my lips and tasted it. We lay like that for a long time, I already losing her and she already going away.

"Now I must get up," she whispered. "I must go now."

"No," I said, "you can't. It's raining; you'll be ill."

"You know I am leaving," she said. "You know I must be alone. I can't stay with other people and live with them."

"You can with me," I said. "You can live with me. You can play with me, can't you, always? I can make things safe for you. We've played together all this time, haven't we, all through the journey?"

"I know." She held my hand. "You are the only one I could live with, but I don't want to. I want to stay alone, and you know it."

Yes, I thought, I know it. "Will you come back?" I asked, but she said she would not come back. And I let her go.

I cried. "It's raining," I said, "it's raining," but she said nothing further. She put both her hands around my neck and kissed me lingeringly on the mouth. Then she went outside, and with my hands clutching the door, I watched her go. At times the moon shone on her from behind masses of clouds, and she looked then like a girl who had come from the moon and was going back because she was homesick. I saw this and I called, "You must come back. Come back, it's the same everywhere," until I could no longer see her and I was all alone.

Long afterward, or not so long, I went back to my uncle Alexander.

"Is that you, Philip?" he asked as I entered the garden.

"Yes, Uncle," I said.

"Have you brought me anything?"

"No, Uncle." I said. "I haven't brought you anything.

June–September, 1954